worked as a frozen-chicken thawer, fashion-industry trainee, department-store Santa, TV producer, newspaper columnist and freelance screenwriter. Then in 1985 he wrote his first novel for young people. Now he's one of Australia's favourite children's authors, with a large following in Britain and many other countries. His most successful titles include *Two Weeks with the Queen*, *Wicked!* (with Paul Jennings), *Boy Overboard* and the two stories included in this book, *Belly Flop* and *Water Wings*.

Rave reviews for *Belly Flop* and *Water Wings*:

'Morris Gleitzman is in dazzling form'
Lindsey Fraser, *Scotsman*

'Morris Gleitzman is a very funny writer,
and *Belly Flop* is moving as well as funny' *TES*

'A gripping, amusing and rather moving story'
Mail on Sunday

'A hard-hitting, often nail-biting story'
Independent on Sunday

'Will make you laugh and cry' *Young Telegraph*

R

D1148562

/A

039580

Misery Guts
Worry Warts
Puppy Fat

Blabber Mouth
Sticky Beak
Gift of the Gab

The Other Facts of Life
Second Childhood
Bumface

With Paul Jennings
Wicked!
Deadly!

Toad Rage
Toad Heaven
Toad Away

Boy Overboard
Girl Underground

Two Weeks with the Queen

Worm Story

Adults Only

Teacher's Pet

Morris Gleitzman

Belly Flop and Water Wings

MACMILLAN CHILDREN'S BOOKS

Belly Flop and *Water Wings* first published individually 1996
by Pan Macmillan Publishers Australia.
First published in the UK 1996 and 1997 respectively
by Pan Macmillan Children's Books

This edition published 2006 by Macmillan Children's Books
a division of Macmillan Publishers Limited
20 New Wharf Road, London N1 9RR
Basingstoke and Oxford
www.panmacmillan.com

Associated companies throughout the world

ISBN-13: 978-0-330-44294-7
ISBN-10: 0-330-44294-5

1 3 5 7 9 8 6 4 2

A CIP catalogue record for this book is available from
the British Library.

Printed and bound in Great Britain
by Mackays of Chatham plc, Kent

CONTENTS

Belly Flop

For Mary-Anne

Chapter One

G'day Doug.

It's me, Mitch Webber.

Sorry to interrupt out of the blue like this, but I'm desperate.

Troy and Brent Malley are after me.

They're the toughest kids in town and I've never seen them so ropeable.

It's really Dad they're angry with, but they've decided to take it out on me.

If they catch me I'll be history.

They've got tractor starter handles.

Oh no, I'm getting a cramp in the leg from running.

Doug, I know it's been a long time, but you're the only angel I know.

Help.

My leg cramp's getting worse, Doug.

I can't run much further.

Sorry to pester you, but the Malleys are getting closer.

I know angels have got busy schedules.

I know you're probably in the middle of a dangerous flight or a complicated rescue or morning tea.

I know it must be a real pain having someone chucking their thoughts at you like this without an appointment.

Specially if you've just settled back on a cloud, taken the weight off your wings and slipped your boots off.

But it's really urgent, Doug, honest.

My lungs are nearly cactus.

The Malleys are so near I can hear the snot rattling in Brent's nose.

I need you.

Jeez, that was close.

When I slipped in that horse poo outside the newsagents, I thought I was Malley meat for sure.

Sometimes it's not so bad having small muscles.

If I had big ones like the Malleys, I'd never have been able to squeeze through that hole in the fence.

Troy and Brent are back there now, yelling.

They're arguing about whether to rip a bigger hole in the fence with their hands or climb over.

Once they decide, I'm dingo bait.

I need a hiding place, Doug.

That's the problem with living in a town with only seven shops, one pub, one bank, one service station and no thick forests.

There aren't many good places to hide.

The safe in the bank'd be good, but it's Sunday.

Even if it wasn't, Mum and Dad work there and I wouldn't want to aggravate Dad's stress rash.

It'll have to be the Memorial Park.

Hope my legs can make it.

This town's so remote, even if the Malleys only manage to inflict surface injuries I'll probably still cark it before the air ambulance arrives.

Now I'm up a tree and I can catch my breath, a thought's just hit me.

You probably don't even remember who I am, Doug.

You angels probably look after so many kids the details get fuzzy.

It's Mitch spelt M-I-T-C-H, Webber spelt W-E-B-B-E-R.

I'm the one who got my head stuck in the bars of that cattle truck.

At the Gas 'N' Gobble when I was little.

When I asked you for help you made the driver drop his ice-cream outside the Men's so when he bent down to pick it up he saw my legs dangling under the truck and didn't jump into the cab and roar off and drag me halfway across Australia.

I think I was wearing a blue T-shirt.

It probably had burn marks on it from when I did that magic trick with the oven lighter and the fluff from under Gran's bed. The one where I asked you to put me out and you made Gavin Sims chuck his milkshake over me.

Do angels have secretaries? If you do, perhaps you could ask yours to jog your memory.

I've thought of trying to get in touch with you heaps of times lately, Doug, but each time I stopped myself on account of me probably being too old now and you probably being up to your neck in angel work.

I'm not stopping myself now, but, because I'm desperate.

You can probably tell that by how hard I'm thinking these thoughts.

And how hard I'm hoping you're receiving them, wherever you are.

Things are pretty crook here, Doug, and I can't manage on my own any more.

I need your help.

I understand if you can't fit me in immediately because you're busy rescuing a little kid from an iceberg or making a crocodile spit out a toddler.

But I'm hoping you're not, Doug.

Because Troy and Brent Malley are over there by the war memorial.

And they've spotted me.

I suppose a tree wasn't such a great hiding place when there are only three in the whole park.

I'm jumping.

I'm rolling in the dust.

I'm running.

Doug, protect me like you used to, please.

I thought I was a goner then.

If I'd taken another half a second getting across the main street that road train would have flattened me.

I'm not sure what'd be worse, being pounded by Troy and Brent Malley or being flattened by a ninety-tonne road train.

I was glad it came along, but.

The Malleys had to wait for it to pass, which gave me time to duck in here.

The dunnies at the Gas 'N' Gobble.

It's OK, Doug, it's not as obvious a hiding place as it sounds.

I'm a boy and I'm in the Ladies.

If anyone comes in I'll tell them I'm looking for the cigarette lighter Gran lost a couple of months ago.

Hang about, Doug.

Of course.

If you don't remember me, you must remember Gran.

She was the one who told me about you, when I was little.

She's tall and sort of wrinkled and she's got a bad . . .

Oh no.

The Malleys are next door in the Men's.

They've heard me panting for breath.

Here we go again.

I've never been that good at athletics, but I reckon if sprinting through a service station and jumping over petrol pump hoses was a school event, I'd be in with a chance.

Specially if I had very angry twins chasing me.

I thought Mr Kee the manager was gunna grab me, but he just stood there with his mouth open.

He didn't even say anything when Troy ran into a car door and dented it.

Or when Brent tripped over the air hose and landed in someone's shopping.

For a sec, when I glanced back, I thought that was you making all that happen, Doug.

Then I remembered what Gran used to tell me about you.

'He's not like one of those posh guardian

angels in the Bible,' she used to say. 'Doug's invisible, he doesn't do violence and he's very busy, so if you need him you've got to ask.'

I'm asking now, Doug.

The Malleys are getting close again.

I can hear them yelling round the corner.

I've just ducked down the side of Conkey's Store, but I doubt if that'll throw them for long.

You're probably wondering, Doug, why I'm not asking anyone around here for help.

Why I'm not running into houses and yelling 'neighbourhood watch' or something.

Things have changed since I last gave you a hoi, Doug.

Everyone in town hates me now.

They hate Dad and Mum and Gran too.

I'll explain why when I've finished climbing up into Mr Conkey's old storage shed.

Chapter Two

Sorry that took a while, Doug.

It's really hard climbing wood when it's rotting.

I'm hoping the Malleys won't think of looking all the way up here in the rafters.

With a bit of luck.

Or rather with a bit of help from you, Doug.

Luck's something we haven't had much of around here lately.

Remember how last time you were round this way it hadn't rained for nearly four years? Well, we haven't had a sprinkle for eight years now, except for a few drops last January which everyone reckoned was from a leaky dunny on a Qantas jet.

It's a really crook drought, everyone says so.

Sheena Bullock's dog can unscrew after-shave bottles with its teeth, that's how crook a drought it is.

Everyone's suffering, but Dad's copping it the worst.

Remember how he used to be one of the most popular blokes in town, partly because of his sweet nature and partly because drought-struck farmers knew that if they came to see Dad he'd make sure the bank lent them some money to keep them going?

Well now everyone hates him.

Someone spat on him in the street yesterday. It was terrible. They'd been eating beetroot.

I've tried to explain to people that Dad's just doing his job.

That it's what a Bank Liaison Officer has to do, write reports on families who are going broke because the drought's killed their sheep and dried up their paddocks.

That's it's not his fault the bank gets twitchy when broke families can't pay back the money they've borrowed.

That it's not his fault the bank takes their farms instead.

I've told people a million times how much Dad hates writing those reports.

How he wishes he could be a swimming pool attendant like Grandad used to be.

How he'd give his right arm to . . .

Hang on, what's that noise?

~

9

For a sec I thought it was the Malleys climbing up to get me.

Relax, Doug, it was just the wooden beams expanding in the heat.

I'm lying stretched out on a rafter now so even if Troy and Brent do come into the shed they definitely won't be able to see me up here under the roof.

Where was I?

Oh, yes.

I'm always reminding people that Dad's the same kind bloke he was before the drought. Reminding them how he nursed the Bullocks' dog back to health after we found it in our backyard with bubbles coming out of its mouth.

But every time the bank chucks a family off their land, everyone blames Dad.

I tell them he's as upset about it as they are.

He is, he's got flaky skin on his upper thighs from the stress. (I don't tell them that.)

I tell them it's the bank bosses in the city that chuck people off their land, not Dad.

But they don't listen.

They just turn away and pretend I'm a bus stop.

Which is pretty hurtful, cause our town hasn't got any bus stops.

People are starting to hate Mum too, and all she does is work in the bank and cash drought-relief cheques and make cups of tea for people who are depressed and upset at the state of their sheep.

The bank offered to promote her to manager, but she said no cause she knew she'd cop it even worse.

Even Gran gets picked on when she goes shopping.

Well, she reckons she does.

She reckons someone muttered to her in Conkey's yesterday how they were going to slit her throat and reach in and pull her intestines out, but she was standing next to a noisy soft drink cabinet and her hearing's not the best.

Anyway, Gran's pretty tough.

It's Dad I'm most worried about, Doug.

If kids chuck my bag on the roof I can climb up and get it, but Dad can't if his clients do that to him. He's too overweight to be a good climber, plus he's meant to be resting his thighs.

The other kids do chuck my bag around a fair bit.

I reckon they hate me almost as much as their parents hate Dad.

I've tried not to think about it too much.

Until this arvo.

I nipped down to Conkey's for some corn chips.

Troy and Brent Malley were waiting for me.

When I saw the expressions on their faces and the tractor starter handles in their hands, I knew my worst nightmare had come true.

If only Dad had warned me the bank was gunna chuck the Malleys off their land.

I could have taken precautions.

Like staying indoors.

And I wouldn't have had to disturb you, Doug.

Sorry if I'm messing up your work schedule and causing you job-related stress, but I'm ...

Listen.

It's that noise again.

That's not beams expanding, that's ...

Oh, no.

Doug.

The Malleys are up here.

They must have climbed up the back of the shed.

They've just stepped out from behind an old crate and they're coming towards me along the rafter.

Grinning.

Their grins are even scarier than their scowls.

Doug, help, I'm on a thin strip of wood miles from the ground being stalked by killer twins.

There's only one thing I can do.

Jump onto the next rafter.

Doug, if you're there, could you give me a sign?

So I know you're looking after me and I won't fall and get mashed.

Just something small.

A thumbs up made of dust floating in the air.

A spider winking at me.

Anything.

Too late.

The Malleys are lunging at me.

I'm jumping.

I've made it.

I'm on the other rafter.

No I'm not.

The wood's splintering.

I'm falling.

Doug . . .

I'm not dead.

I can move both my arms.

And both my legs.

And most of my bottom.

Doug, you did it.

You broke my fall.

Jeez, I'd forgotten how good you are at this angel caper.

It must take years of training to make a

person who's falling that distance land exactly on a pile of empty cardboard boxes and not on the concrete floor or the rusty old sheep feed machine.

Thanks, Doug.

Troy and Brent can't believe it.

They're staring down with their jaws hanging loose.

Even from this far away I can see that their faces have gone pale and their legs are quivering.

They look like stunned sheep.

I'm shaking too.

On the inside as well.

My heart and liver and guts are quivering more than the stuff in the butcher's window when a cattle truck goes past.

Not because of the fall, Doug.

Because I'm so happy and excited.

You've come back.

Chapter Three

It's amazing, Doug.

Now I'm a client of yours again, I feel totally different.

I can even run faster.

I've just made it home in a couple of ticks and the Malleys weren't even in sight.

Thanks, Doug.

Thank you.

Thank you.

Thank you.

This is the best birthday present I've ever had.

Did I mention today's my birthday?

That's why I'm catching my breath on the front verandah.

I don't want to burst into the house panting and looking like I've just been chased three times round town by a pair of psychopaths.

Mum and Dad have got enough stress as it is.

And they're about to have some more.

My birthday party starts in twenty minutes

and there's something about it I haven't told them yet.

Something very important.

I haven't been game to tell them in case they chucked a fit.

But now you're back, Doug, it'll be fine.

What I've got to tell them is that my birthday party's not just a birthday party.

It's the event that's gunna make everything in our lives OK again.

When I got inside, Gran was having a go at Dad as usual.

'Three more families heaved off their land by that bank of yours,' she was saying. 'Don't take it personally, but I reckon you're lower than the flap of skin on a sheep's rear end.'

Dad was ignoring her as usual and pretending to look for something in his briefcase.

'Mum,' said Mum wearily to Gran, 'do us all a favour and change the subject, eh?'

Gran got herself a beer.

Mum plonked a bowl of taco dip down with the other party food and then saw me.

'Mitch,' she said, 'we were wondering where you were. Did you get the extra corn chips?'

I tried desperately to think of an answer that wasn't a lie.

'Couldn't,' I said. 'Sorry.'

Mum ran a worried eye over the food table.

'Oh well,' she said, 'we should have enough.'

I took a deep breath.

I don't know if you were ever a kid, Doug, but if you were you'll know how hard it can be telling your parents stuff that might hinder their breathing.

'Mum,' I said, 'I've invited some extra kids to the party.'

Mum frowned.

'I thought we agreed,' she said. 'Five or six and no horses in the house.'

'Too many and it'll put a strain on the furniture,' said Dad, 'and the dunny.'

I took another deep breath.

'I've invited a few more than five or six,' I said.

'How many?' said Gran through a mouthful of peanuts.

'Seventy-three,' I said.

Mum dropped a plate of chocolate crackles.

Dad went so stressed he looked like a city person.

Gran had a coughing fit and sprayed peanuts across the room.

'I did it for all of us,' I said, banging Gran on the back. 'So we can show them our human side.'

Mum and Dad stared at me.

17

'That's why I asked you to rehearse your card tricks, Gran,' I went on, 'and you to learn some good jokes, Mum, and you to practise juggling ping-pong balls with your mouth, Dad. When all the kids see how much fun we are at parties, they'll tell their parents and everyone'll stop hating us so much.'

Dad jumped out of his chair so fast you'd never guess he's a bit overweight.

'Mitch,' he said, grabbing me and knocking the tomato sauce bottle over, 'stop that talk. The people in this town don't hate us. They just get crook with me because of my job. They certainly don't hate you. You're a good kid and it's just your bad luck to have me as a dad.'

I couldn't speak, partly because what he'd just said had made my throat go funny and partly because he was gripping my shoulders so hard.

If I hadn't already known him I'd have been amazed to discover he was a Bank Liaison Officer and not a professional arm wrestler.

There was another pause while Gran wiped tomato sauce off the jelly and Mum gave Dad a worried squeeze.

Then I told Dad he was wrong about the bad luck and that he was the only dad I'd ever want, even if we lived in a huge city where there were millions of other dads.

I put my arms round him as far as I could and gave him a hug.

He is wrong, but.

Not just about me, about all of us.

We're the most hated family in the district.

Dad knows it.

That's why a tear ran down his face and sploshed into Gran's beer.

And that's why I've invited every kid in town to my party.

Chapter Four

We're all sitting here watching the chocolate crackles melt and waiting for the kids to arrive.

They should be here any minute.

Mum and Dad have just had a private conversation in the kitchen and they don't seem so worried now about the extra kids.

When Mum and Dad came back in I had a thought.

'Let's drag my bed in,' I said, 'for the kids at the back to stand on so they can see the card tricks and the ping-pong balls.'

Mum and Dad looked at each other.

I think they could see the sense in it.

'And we'd better put some more mashed baked beans in the taco dip,' I said.

'Good idea,' said Mum. 'We'll do it after they get here.'

Dad nodded and spilled his tea.

I think we're all pretty excited.

Except Gran.

She seems to be frowning a lot, though that

could because her cigarette ash has dropped
down inside her bra.

They shouldn't be much longer now, Doug.
   You probably think I'm a bit mental, having
a party when everyone hates me.
   I'm not.
   I've thought about this for weeks and I
reckon it's a good plan.
   You work with kids, Doug, so be honest.
   What kid can resist a party?
   None in this town, it's a known fact.
   Plus I've made it really easy for them.
   I hand-delivered the invitations to their
school lockers so they wouldn't have to make
conversation with me.
   I chose three o'clock as the starting time so
they wouldn't have to gobble their lunch.
   And I made it fancy dress so they could
come in disguise if they were embarrassed to
be seen here.
   They'll arrive soon, you wait and see.
   Oops.
   Gran's choking on a Cheezel.
   I'd better go and bang her on the back.

Hope you don't mind me sending my
thoughts to you like this, Doug.
   It helps me keep my mind off the clock.
   If me yakking on like this is making it hard

for you to concentrate on saving any of the other kids on your roster, don't listen, OK?

It's twenty-seven past three.

Mum and Dad are looking a bit stressed.

Pity angels only do rescues.

We could do with something to break the tension and give us a laugh.

One of the balloons popping or Dad sitting on the pikelets or something.

Dad's been showing me the features of the calculator they gave me for my birthday.

'Look,' he said, 'it calculates loan repayments to six decimal places.'

Gran had a coughing fit.

I decided I'd better try and help everyone relax.

'Don't worry,' I said, 'the kids have probably been held up.'

'I doubt it,' said Gran, 'seeing as it only takes thirteen and a half minutes to walk from one end of town to the other, fourteen in a dust storm.'

Poor old Gran.

She gets a bit grumpy sometimes.

It's from being ancient.

I reckon she's remarkable for her age, but she does have one habit that gets her into a bit of strife.

Remember how she's always been a heavy smoker, Doug?

Well now she eats while she does it.

I don't blame her, but.

If I was in my twilight years I'd want to pack as much as I could into each moment too. I'd probably do something dopey like watch videos in the shower.

There goes Gran now, puffing away and choking on a chocolate crackle.

She's always choking on chocolate crackles.

It's her fault, she knows she should pour hot milk on them first. She knows they don't get soft enough when she dips them in her beer.

What makes it worse is she's pretty tall for an old person so she's got long pipes. That means when food gets stuck it's got a fair distance to travel and she needs a lot of thumps on the back.

It's OK but, she's pretty solid.

S'cuse me Doug.

It's nineteen minutes to four.

Mum and Dad are looking very stressed.

Dad's put his elbow in his beer three times.

A couple of secs ago a thought hit me.

Perhaps they're worried that when the kids arrive, they might all try to bash me up.

'It's OK,' I said, 'if things get out of hand I can give Doug a hoi.'

Mum and Dad looked at each other and pretended they hadn't heard.

'I probably won't have to,' I said, 'but he's around if I need him.'

Gran coughed a Cheezel across the room.

Mum and Dad looked at each other again and I could tell from their pained expressions they'd heard.

That's when I remembered.

Don't be offended Doug, but Mum and Dad don't believe in you.

It's one of their few real faults.

If they can't see a person, and offer them a cup of tea or something cold, they don't believe in them.

Try not to hold it against them, Doug.

It's seventeen minutes to four.

If a spaceship's landed in Memorial Park and everyone's down there, you'd let me know, eh Doug?

It's OK, Doug, I'm not crying.

My eyes are just a bit drippy, that's all.

Us humans get drippy eyes sometimes if we're tired or we've been watching too much telly or we get toothpaste in them.

Or we have a birthday party and nobody comes.

I still can't believe it.

I wasn't expecting every kid in town to trample the door down, but I thought some'd turn up even if it was just to see Gran cough bits of corn chip out of her nose.

Not a single one.

Not even Andy Howard, who'd normally walk naked through bull ants for a free feed.

Poor old Mum and Dad, it was good of them to try and cheer me up, even if they aren't very good at it.

Just now, when Mum said 'Never mind, love, they've probably got the wrong day', and Dad stared at the Cheezel on top of the TV and said 'They'll probably turn up next Sunday', I had to bite my tongue really hard.

I wanted to yell something really angry.

Something about how some parents' jobs make it really hard for a kid to have a birthday party.

I still do, but Gran's coughing and they probably won't hear me.

Anyway, it wouldn't be fair.

Dad can't help . . .

What was that?

Doug, quick.

The window just exploded.

There's glass everywhere.

What's happening?

Is someone shooting at us?

Are there farmers out there with guns?

Doug.

Help.

HELP.

Chapter Five

It's OK Doug, it was just a brick.

Don't get me wrong.

That's bad enough.

We've never had a brick before and we're all shaking like a truckie's gut.

But at least it's not as bad as a bullet.

I just wish I'd seen it coming, then I could have got you to stop it.

But I didn't see it till it had smashed through the window.

The noise made us freeze and we just sat there like stunned fish fillets watching the brick land in the Cheezels and bits of glass bounce off the walls and tinkle across the floor.

Then everyone moved.

Mum dived protectively across Gran.

It was good of her, but a bit of a waste of time cause she's about half the size of Gran and her skin is still quite soft except for her elbows and Gran's is like leather-grain vinyl.

Still, you can't blame her for trying.

She's got diving in her blood from Grandad.

Poor old Dad hasn't.

When he tried to throw himself protectively on top of me he got the angle wrong and bounced off the rocker recliner and landed on the food table.

That's when I unfroze and yelled for you, Doug.

I know guardian angels are really only meant to protect kids, so it was good of you to make sure Dad's head missed the cutlery and landed on something soft.

All those swear words he came out with while we were getting the taco dip out of his eyes weren't about you, I promise.

They were about the person who chucked the brick.

We're out in the street now, but we can't see anyone.

Doesn't matter.

We know who did it, don't we Doug?

I've just told Mum and Dad about Troy and Brent Malley.

They were pretty shocked.

Mum gave me a hug.

Dad looked as though he was going to cry, though that might have been because of what he'd just seen.

27

My calculator.

Smashed to bits.

Dad reckons we mustn't jump to conclusions, but.

He could be right.

I've just noticed something scratched on the brick.

The word MONGREL.

I'm not sure if Troy and Brent Malley can spell that well.

Dad's on the phone now giving Sergeant Crean a list of the people he reckons would chuck a brick through our window. Dad hates dobbing, but he's had to mention most of the town.

I'm still shaking, Doug.

My guts feel like they've been through a sheep feed machine.

Mum's still shaking too. Even her shoulders are trembling, and I don't think it's because she's picking up broken glass. She's normally very relaxed handling sharp objects, that's why she's so good at darts.

Gran usually shakes a bit, but not as much as she is now.

She wouldn't admit it, but I think she's a bit scared. You can tell by the words she's yelling at Dad.

'Get a different job, Hopeless, before we're all killed,' for example.

Normally she's much ruder to him than that.

Mum and Dad have gone to give a statement about the brick to Sergeant Crean down at the bowls club.

Poor things.

It won't be easy for them, walking into that place with everyone throwing glances at them and muttering things.

I'm on my bed trying to fit my calculator back together.

It's not easy with my hands shaking so much.

Gran's just been in.

'Good on you for having a punt,' she said.

At first I thought she meant the calculator.

I'd just spent ten minutes trying to straighten a bent battery terminal and wondering if angels are any good at electrical repairs.

She didn't.

'That was a brave try, the party,' she said. 'You had a punt, that's the main thing.'

Gran reckons if a person won't have a punt, they might as well just lie down and let a cattle truck run over them.

'Thanks, Gran,' I said.

She went to her room for a rest.

Poor thing.

She's too old to be hated by an entire town.

Specially when her and Grandad used to be so popular.

Once Gran was president of the bowls club four years in a row.

And Grandad, before he died, was the most loved swimming pool attendant this town's ever had.

And the best diver.

It says so on his retirement medal.

The one Mum keeps in her bedside drawer for when she needs a cry.

I'm gunna stop wasting my time on this calculator, Doug.

I've got more important stuff to do.

Like come up with another plan to make everything in our lives OK again.

Chapter Six

Last night wasn't a good night for coming up with plans.

My brain kept getting distracted by other stuff.

Worrying about school today, mostly.

Having to face all those kids.

Specially two of them in particular.

I'd have been awake all night if it hadn't been for you, Doug.

When I was little and Gran used to tell me about you, she always reckoned guardian angels were better than hot milk drinks for getting to sleep.

She was right.

Thanks, Doug.

I feel a bit better about the Malleys this morning.

I think it's because I dreamed about you, just like I used to.

Boy, I was glad to see you.

Well, not actually see you of course, but feel your breeze.

It was a top dream.

I was in the main street and I was pretty upset, partly cause Dad had just stuck his elbow in my ice-cream and partly cause the town was surrounded by hundreds of angry farmers with guns who wanted to kill us.

Me and Dad knew we were history.

Even if we ran as fast as we could, there was no way we'd make it to Conkey's, buy guns for ourselves, unwrap them and load them before the farmers started firing.

I wanted Dad to hold my hand tight, but he was busy wiping peach and mango ripple off his elbow.

Then the posters started flapping outside the newsagents and I knew it was you, Doug.

As usual you were amazing. In less than thirty seconds the farmers remembered some urgent fence repairs they had to do and went home in an orderly manner.

And I've woken up with a really good feeling.

That ripper peaceful feeling of knowing you're looking after me.

Emergency call to Doug.

Emergency call to Doug.

Dad's in a bad way.

I've never seen him so clumsy.

He usually has one accident on his way to

the car, maybe two, but I've never seen him have four.

Getting his keys tangled up in his hanky, dropping his briefcase, tripping over the garden hose and banging his knee on the carport all on the same morning'd be a record, I'd say.

I was at the mail box when he came a cropper over the hose, which he'd have to be pretty tense to do as it's been in the same spot untouched for eight years.

Then, when he was in the car, I understood.

Mum came out and before she got in the car herself she asked him if he needed some goanna oil for his knee.

'I'll be right,' he said. 'I'll just be doing desk work most of the day. I'm not due out at the Malleys with their eviction papers till three.'

My insides plummeted.

I went stiff with shock.

If there had been any birthday cards for me I'd probably have dropped them.

Mr and Mrs Malley are just as muscly as Troy and Brent, and taller, and they own about six guns each.

They shoot things for fun, not just sick sheep.

Doug, I know you're busy and I know guardian angels are really only meant to look after kids, but could you keep an eye on Dad this arvo?

33

He needs you, Doug.

Don't worry about me.

I'll have come up with a plan by then to win the hearts of everyone in town, including Troy and Brent Malley.

I know I will.

Thanks, Doug.

By the time I got to school I was so tense I couldn't think straight.

I couldn't stop imagining Dad's bullet-riddled body stuffed in the Malleys' sock drawer.

It took me a couple of minutes to notice Troy and Brent weren't around.

Even then I had the awful thought that perhaps they'd been kept at home to help load the guns so Mr and Mrs Malley won't have to stop to do it this arvo and lose concentration while they're shooting at Dad.

Then I realised it wasn't that, it was you, Doug.

You've made Troy and Brent late so I can get into class in one piece.

Simple and clever.

Which is also how I'd describe the idea I've just had, even though I say it myself.

It came to me while I was hanging up my bag.

I saw the permission form for the school excursion sticking out the top.

Have I told you about the school excursion?

A school way over on the coast has invited our school to go and take part in their swimming carnival on account of us being drought-struck. Someone must have told them about us not having any water in our town pool for the last eight years.

I was meant to get Mum or Dad to fill out the form over the weekend.

Poop, I thought when I saw it, and started filling it out myself.

Then the idea hit me.

The bus trip to the coast is gunna take about a million hours.

Kids get bored to death on buses.

So I'll have my party on the bus.

Pretty good, eh?

Most of the party food'll keep in the freezer till then and I can get Mum and Gran and Dad to teach me the jokes and card tricks and ping-pong ball juggling.

I'm on my way into class now.

I can't wait to tell everyone.

I reckon they'll be really grateful.

They'd have to really hate someone to knock back the chance of a long bus trip with no boredom and heaps of chocolate crackles and taco dip.

I don't reckon even they hate me that much.

~

They hate me that much.

I remembered they did the moment I walked into class and saw them all crowded round my desk.

And saw what was waiting for me.

A present, wrapped in shiny paper with a frilly bow.

And a card saying 'Happy Birthday Webface, hope you had a good party.'

I'd have ignored it if Mr Tristos hadn't walked in at that moment and seen it.

'Mitch,' he said, looking surprised, 'you're popular today.'

The kids started chanting 'Open it! Open it!'

I gave Mr Tristos a pleading look.

He doesn't usually let kids open presents in class and I was hoping desperately he'd stop me.

'Go on, Mitch,' he said, 'open it.'

Then I remembered that last year the bank chucked his wife's parents off their farm.

The kids cheered and Mr Tristos said he reckoned it was socks and the kids kacked themselves.

The smell hit me while I was still undoing the ribbon, but I carried on even though I knew before the paper fell open and the kids went hysterical that it was dog poo.

I pretended I wasn't hurt.

36

Mr Tristos pretended to explode with rage.

'Whoever brought this into class,' he yelled, 'will be punished,' but I could see his heart wasn't in it.

If he'd really wanted to punish someone he'd have kept the poo as evidence instead of taking it outside and chucking it in the bin.

In a town where the dogs are as friendly as this one, dog poo can be identified pretty easily.

I only got to look at it for a few seconds before my eyes got hot and my vision went blurry, and even after that short time I had the suspects narrowed down to a shortlist of three.

It doesn't matter.

A party on a bus was a dopey idea.

I'm just grateful I've realised that now instead of on the excursion.

Because now I've got the chance to come up with a better plan.

Doug, help.

We're handing in our permission forms and when I turned just now to give mine to Mr Tristos, I saw them.

Troy and Brent Malley.

They're outside the window, staring at me.

Even their freckles are scowling.

What makes it worse is that their eyes are red.

Jeez, if the bank's made them cry I'm in deep poop.

Everyone knows the Malleys don't cry.

Perhaps it's just dust. Their Dad's ute hasn't got side windows.

Except if it is dust, why are they looking at the playground where we all have to go at lunchtime and then back at me and mouthing words that almost all look like they begin with the letter F?

I'm trying to give them a friendly smile.

It's not easy.

My mouth doesn't want to smile, it wants to shout 'help'.

Troy and Brent aren't smiling back.

They're swinging their school bags over their shoulders like they probably do with wild pigs they've shot or bashed up and now they're going down to their classroom.

I'm desperately trying to think what to do, Doug.

I could offer to find Mr and Mrs Malley other work, but I don't think that'd calm Troy and Brent down.

Not even if I offer to write to Hollywood and see if they can fit Mr and Mrs Malley into their next movie as hired guns.

I hope you're receiving this, Doug, and I hope you're not busy in seventeen minutes.

That's when the lunch bell goes.

Chapter Seven

The lunch bell's just gone, Doug.

I've squeezed my brain into turnip mash trying to work out how you can save me.

All I've come up with is you appearing in the playground and dazzling Troy and Brent with flying tricks and possibly some juggling.

Which shows how panicked I am.

I know perfectly well you're invisible so you won't show up on air traffic controllers' radar screens and so your work won't be hindered by adoring crowds trying to mob you.

Hang on, what's this?

A Year Two kid sticking her head round the door and yelling that Mrs Stegnjaaic in the office wants to see me.

You're a genius, Doug.

I wouldn't have thought of something as brilliantly simple as that in a million years.

How do you come up with stuff like that?

Do angels have to study and take exams, or

is it just a skill that develops naturally like pig shooting?

Either way, it's working.

If I keep my head down and keep on walking fast, in fifteen seconds I'll be in the office and Troy and Brent'll be scratching their heads in the playground thinking I've turned invisible.

Don't stop what you're doing, Doug.

If you're in the middle of something important like finding a kid lost in the desert without a hat, ignore me.

But if you can spare half an ear, you might be interested to hear how things went in the office.

Just like you planned, that's how.

Usually people are only called to the office for family emergencies, so I was half expecting Mrs Stegnjaaic to say something like 'your mum and dad are being held captive in the bank by a gang of armed farmers' or 'your gran accidentally set fire to a plate of chocolate crackles and burnt the house down'.

I was quite surprised when all she did was hold up my excursion permission form and say 'we need more information'.

For a sec I thought she meant more information about the excursion.

I wouldn't have put that past you Doug,

getting me away from the Malleys by having Mrs Stegnjaaic send me on a special three-day trip over to the coast to find out if the school there's got lockers.

Then I realised she meant more information about the name I'd put on the form under Next of Kin.

Your name, Doug.

I hope you don't mind.

'This isn't your dad's name,' said Mrs Stegnjaaic.

My heart started going a bit wobbly.

I explained that Mum and Dad have got a lot on their plate at the moment.

Mrs Stegnjaaic looked sympathetic. She can be really kind and understanding, not like Ms Dorrit the principal.

'Doug's not enough,' said Mrs Stegnjaaic. 'We need a full name and phone number.'

'Um,' I said, 'that's a bit difficult.'

At that moment Ms Dorrit came out of her office.

'Are you being a pest species again, Mitch Webber?' she said.

I shook my head and Mrs Stegnjaaic said I wasn't and explained the situation.

'So what's the problem?' said Ms Dorrit, turning back to me. 'Why can't you give us this Doug's full name, address and phone number?'

I told her I don't know what they are.

Ms Dorrit's eyes narrowed, which happens when she thinks kids are having a lend of her.

'Who exactly is this person?' she said in a voice that made my neck prickle.

I tried to swallow but my throat felt even more drought-struck than the district.

'A close friend,' I said.

Ms Dorrit's eyes narrowed so much I started worrying that if she tried to leave the room she'd walk into the filing cabinet.

'Perhaps,' she said, in a voice that grated almost as much as the gearbox on the council water truck, 'he could pop in and give us the information himself.'

I felt sick.

Ms Dorrit's eyes were stabbing into me.

'It's a bit tricky,' I said. 'He's invisible.'

Ms Dorrit took a deep breath.

She looked at me for ages.

'In other words,' she said, 'he doesn't exist.'

I couldn't help it, Doug.

I had to say it.

'Yes he does,' I said. 'He's my guardian angel.'

Ms Dorrit looked like she'd just swallowed a filling.

I explained to her how angels can't hang around all day because they've got other kids to protect and how you're squeezing me into your schedule as it is.

'Wouldn't be fair on the other kids to drag him back,' I said, 'just for paperwork.'

There was a snigger from the doorway.

We all turned.

Gavin Sims was standing there smirking.

Ms Dorrit told him to wait outside.

Then she turned back to me.

'Alright Mitch Webber,' she said in her death voice, 'enough of this nonsense. For wasting our time you can stand here, outside my office, silently, for the rest of lunch.'

I know I'm a dope, Doug, but for a fleeting second I panicked.

The awful thought hit me that perhaps you'd had to dash off somewhere so fast you hadn't had time to come up with anything to protect me after all.

Mrs Stegnjaaic gave me a sympathetic look and went back to her typing.

Then I saw Troy and Brent Malley staring at me through the window, their faces bulging with frustration.

Which turned to fear when Ms Dorrit went out and yelled at them and sent them away from the window.

That's when I realised I'm not being looked after by just any old angel, I'm being looked after by the top angel in the whole world, possibly the universe.

Getting me kept in for the whole of lunch

is one of the best things anyone's ever done for me.

Thanks, Doug.

Class has only just started after lunch and Mr Tristos has yelled at me already.

For daydreaming.

He was wrong.

I wasn't daydreaming.

I was coming up with another plan.

Doug, when you're keeping an eye on Dad at the Malleys' place this arvo, don't worry about Troy and Brent bashing me up.

I want them to.

It's OK, I haven't gone mental.

I reckon the kids at this school aren't as mean as they make out.

I reckon underneath they've got pretty good hearts.

And when they see Troy and Brent pounding me into dingo bait, I reckon they're gunna feel pretty sorry for me and realise this drought's tough on me and my family too.

OK, perhaps not dingo bait exactly.

Perhaps just a few cuts and bruises, Doug, and possibly a black eye as long as there's no loss of vision.

Chapter Eight

There's a frog that can live under the ground for nine years without coming up once to stretch its legs or have a pee.

We're doing it in class now.

When a drought starts it burrows down into the desert and stays there till things improve.

I wish I could do the same, Doug.

Not cause I'm scared.

Cause I'm ashamed.

Ashamed of my class and my teacher.

I reckon Mr Tristos must have damaged his hearing at the staff karaoke night.

When twenty-seven kids spend a whole afternoon making rude and insulting jokes about a person's guardian angel and the teacher doesn't hear any of them, that teacher should be thinking about major ear surgery.

Please accept my apologies, Doug, for my very rude class and a teacher who's obviously scared of doctors.

I know who told everyone.

Gavin Sims.

I reckon that's crook, eavesdropping on a private conversation between a person and a principal and then blabbing about it.

I'm turning round now and giving him the look you give ex-friends who've betrayed you.

He's smirking, but I bet he's tortured with guilt inside.

The other kids are still whispering and laughing.

I'm going to ignore them.

And I will, just as soon as Matthew Conn stops singing that dumb song about fairies.

This is only a thought, Doug, because you're the expert, but I reckon he'd shut up pretty quick if he found he'd accidentally stapled his tongue to the desk.

OK Doug, I know I shouldn't have had that thought about Matthew Conn's tongue.

It was too cruel, plus he doesn't have a stapler.

I'm glad you didn't do anything to him, or any of the others.

That means you're ignoring them just like I am.

Which is what they deserve.

It'd be tragic if their mean and vicious behaviour distracted you from doing any medical miracles or freeing any kids from terrorists' hideouts.

Or protecting Dad in a few minutes.

That's why I'm glad you're not letting yourself be distracted at the moment while Mr Tristos is out taking a phone call and Danielle Wicks is standing on my desk flapping her arms.

I reckon she's only doing it to impress Carla Fiami.

Carla's ignoring her, like me.

OK, I have got a few tears in my eyes, but that's normal when you're in a hated family.

No big deal.

Except I am having second thoughts about letting the Malleys bash me up.

I don't reckon these kids are capable of feeling sorry for a person.

Not unless that person's got internal injuries and an ear ripped off, and I'm just not prepared to go that far.

Don't worry Doug, I've worked out how to make it home without Troy and Brent Malley getting me.

I've just remembered a very wise thing Gran once told me.

'Tough kids,' she said, 'usually can't run as fast as scared kids.'

She's right, as long as the scared kids get a decent start.

47

Chapter Nine

As soon as the bell went I was out of my seat, out of the room and first to the pegs.

But even as I was grabbing my bag I heard someone come up behind me.

My heart started thumping louder than a water pipe when the tank's empty.

I turned round.

It wasn't Troy Malley.

Or Brent.

It was Carla Fiami.

My heart kept thumping.

Carla Fiami may not be as tough as the Malleys but she's almost as vicious.

And she does most of it with words.

'Bit slack, this dopey guardian angel of yours, eh?' she said.

Carla's got very black eyes with curly hair hanging over them and they glint in a way that makes most people really nervous.

I thought of explaining that you're not slack, Doug, just busy, but I didn't.

I reckoned she was just filling in time till the Malleys arrived so she could make sarcastic comments about their punching technique while they pounded me into sheep pellets.

Instead she grabbed me and said 'Come on' and dragged me outside.

I wanted to sprint for the gate, but it was too late.

Kids were coming out of all the other classrooms, including Troy and Brent's.

Carla dragged me round the back of the school hall.

'Climb up,' she said.

I stared at her.

The only way up was the drainpipe, but it collapsed ages ago when Paul Keighley's big brother tried to climb it and it's been leaning against the wall ever since.

Carla pushed it to one side.

Behind it, hanging from the gutter bracket, was a rope.

'Climb up and lie on the roof till they've gone,' said Carla. 'I did it last week when Ms Dorrit was after me. Or are you scared of heights?'

I opened my mouth to tell her that one of my ancestors could do backward dives off the high board at the town pool, then decided it wasn't a good time.

I started climbing the rope.

Carla gave me a push up.

'Guardian angel,' she snorted. 'You must be a complete dope.'

It wasn't a good time for an argument either, but I had to say something.

'No I'm not,' I said.

'Dreamland,' she said. 'Get real.'

'What makes you the expert?' I said.

'I had a guardian angel for seven years,' she said, 'then he dumped me.'

I almost fell off the rope.

I opened my mouth to ask her at least fifty questions but she told me to save my breath for climbing.

After nearly bursting both lungs and a kneecap, I finally got up here on the roof and stared down at her.

'Why?' I panted.

She didn't get my drift.

I meant why did her guardian angel dump her, but Carla thought I meant why was she helping me.

'Cause you invited me to your party,' she said. 'I couldn't come cause I was busy, plus I wouldn't be seen dead at your place, but thanks.'

Before I could say anything she ran off.

I can't stop thinking about what she said.

Even though I'm lying on scorching tin and I can hear Troy and Brent Malley looking for me down below, I can't keep my mind off it.

Dumped by an angel.

That's tragic.

She must have done something really bad.

Doug, when you've finished keeping an eye on Dad, could you get in touch with Carla's ex-angel and have a quick word with him or her and explain that even though Carla's got a hurtful tongue and a mean way of looking at people she's actually a pretty nice person inside.

Thanks, Doug.

I won't interrupt again.

I was wrong, Doug, I'm interrupting again.

Troy and Brent Malley have found the rope.

I can hear them climbing.

They'll be up here on the roof in about ten seconds.

I haven't got a knife to cut the rope.

It'll take me at least half an hour to bite through it.

I dunno what to do.

If I jump I'll be history.

If they get their hands on me I'll be dingo bait.

Doug, help.

Chapter Ten

That's better.

I'm not seeing double any more and my nose has stopped bleeding.

Once my knee stops swelling and the headache goes, I'll be pretty right.

I'm a lucky bloke.

Lucky to have you, Doug.

Without you I could have been really injured.

I'm also lucky the school hall's got high windows.

And that the teacher who had gym this arvo left the gym mats piled up.

Jeez, it was close but.

When I finally got a window open wide enough to climb through, Brent Malley was so near I could hear the saliva flapping in his windpipe.

If I hadn't jumped when I did, he'd have got a firmer grip on my leg and I'd never have been able to shake him off.

As it was he knocked me off balance, which is why I jumped head first.

And why I did the double somersault on the way down.

I just wish I could have done two and a half, cause then I'd have landed on my feet instead of my face.

Boy, high dives are faster in real life than on telly. I barely had a chance to yell before it was all over.

I can see why championship divers prefer water to gym mats. If they dived onto gym mats they'd spend half their lives staggering around in a daze dropping their trophies.

And if they ever had to sprint out of a school hall directly afterwards and run for their lives from the Malleys, they'd have real trouble reaching their top speed.

I am.

Thanks Doug, for looking after Dad.

He's just driven past without any visible bullet holes in him or the four-wheel drive.

Jeez, I'm relieved.

I waved and yelled, but he didn't see me.

I wish he had.

I don't know if I can run all the way home with this knee.

Plus I want to tell him about my dive.

I reckon he'd be really proud.

Even Grandad couldn't always do a double somersault.

Most of all I want to tell him about the Malleys' faces after I did it.

For a few secs, before they ran off to climb down and come after me, they stared down through the window.

And guess what, Doug?

They were impressed.

You should have seen their faces, they looked like . . .

Oh, Doug.

I'm having an idea.

Keep my legs moving, Doug, please.

I can feel the blood rushing to my brain.

I think this is the one.

Yes.

Yes.

Yes.

Yes.

Why didn't I think of it before?

I'm gunna become a world champion diver.

Or at least an Australian one.

And when I've won loads of trophies and medals for diving off really high diving boards, and earned heaps of honour and glory for this town, the people round here'll have to feel differently about me.

And Dad.

People always like the dads of sports champions, it's a known fact.

OK, Doug, I know what you're probably thinking.

You're probably thinking I'm pretty dopey deciding to be a diver when there's not a pool, river, creek or dam in these parts with any water in it.

That's the whole point.

If I'm gunna impress people I've got to do something that no one else from this district can do.

I reckon I'm probably the only kid for six hundred thousand square kilometres around here who's planning to be a champion diver.

I've seen championship diving on telly and I know I can do it.

OK, not a triple reverse somersault with twist straight off, but I've already done a double forward somersault, and I reckon I could have added a twist if the Malleys hadn't rushed me.

After all, I've got diving in my blood.

And you to stop me having any tragic accidents, Doug.

If I can teach myself a triple reverse somersault by next week when we go on the swimming carnival excursion, I reckon I can win the diving over there and be off and running on the road to international success.

This is it.

The plan I've been looking for.

Jeez, I'm so excited my legs are going all wobbly.

I can hardly run any more.

I can't see the Malleys, but they can't be far behind.

Quick, Doug, I need a hiding place.

Chapter Eleven

For a sec just then I thought Mr Bullock was gunna chuck me out.

He doesn't like kids hanging round his shop if they're not renting a video.

Thanks, Doug, for making Sheena's dog recognise me and lick me so much that Mr Bullock changed his mind and let me stay.

And thanks for giving me the idea of coming here.

The Action and Horror section in the video store's a great place to hide.

For a start, if I crouch down by this bottom shelf pretending to look for forgotten musicals Arnold Schwarzenegger made before he was a star, I can't be seen from the street.

Plus if anyone comes in they'll most likely go to the Water section rather than this one. Mr Bullock keeps movies with water in them in their own section at the front. *Twenty Thousand Leagues Under the Sea, The River Wild, A Fish Called Wanda,* that sort of stuff. They're the most popular type of videos round here since the drought started.

I must check out the ones with diving in them.

Troy and Brent Malley hate water movies.

All their favourite videos are in Action and Horror.

Everyone knows that.

Troy and Brent would never expect anyone they were after to hide in their section, not in a million years.

Good on you, Doug.

They'll never find me here.

Don't blame yourself, Doug.

It was a fluke, them finding me there.

I reckon they'd given up looking for me and had decided to rent a video with lots of killing in it to make themselves feel better.

Thanks for distracting them so I could duck past them and run for it.

That was a top move, having Mr Bullock call them over to the counter to pick up that copy of *Death on the Nile* their parents had reserved.

With that sort of start I've got a good chance of getting home before they catch me.

As long as I don't stop running.

~

You probably think I was pretty dopey to stop running, Doug.

Perhaps I was.

But it was something I had to do.

Halfway down our street I had a sudden vision of me spending the rest of my life being chased by Troy and Brent Malley and never having a chance to do any diving.

People just don't get to be international diving champs if they're always being knocked off balance by angry twins, it's a known fact.

So I decided to face up to them and get it over with.

The problem was, once I'd stopped and turned round and Troy and Brent had stopped and got over their surprise, everything happened too fast.

Before I could catch my breath and tell them I'd fight them one at a time, they were both on me and Troy was pushing my face in the dirt and kneeing me in the back and Brent was kicking me in the side and giving me Chinese burns on both arms at once.

I know you'd have saved me, Doug, if I'd called.

I still don't know why I didn't.

The Chinese burns must have affected my brain.

All I could think of was a completely dopey idea.

59

That Dad would save me.

I must have been delirious.

Dad isn't that sort of person. He's tried to rescue me a few times, for example the time I accidentally shut myself in the safe at the bank, but he panics and knocks things over and other people have to do it.

Just now but, when Troy and Brent finally stopped thumping me and I realised it was because someone had chucked cold water over us, for a sec I really thought it was Dad.

Yes, I thought, at last he's finally made his arms and legs do what he wants in a time of crisis.

But when I blinked the water out of my eyes it wasn't Dad standing there with a dripping bucket, it was Gran.

I still can't believe it.

Gran can get pretty angry, specially when Mum and Dad try to make her give up smoking or throw Grandad's overalls away, but I've never seen her as ropeable as she was just now.

Her eyes were like glowing cigarette tips, and even though she was wearing her saggy dress, the way she stuck her chest out made her look even taller than usual.

'You two mongrels on your feet,' she yelled at Troy and Brent.

60

They scrambled off me.

'If you want to bash someone for chucking you off your land,' Gran said to them, 'go in there and bash his dad.'

She pointed to our place.

Troy and Brent stared at her.

I stood up quickly in case they accepted her offer, but they didn't.

'Otherwise take a hike,' said Gran, 'and if you go crooked on this bloke again instead of those that deserve it, I'll tear strips off you wide enough to . . .'

Gran stopped for a cough.

Troy and Brent didn't hang around for her to start yelling again.

They wiped the muddy water off their faces and glared at me and ran.

'You OK?' asked Gran when she'd finished having a spit.

I nodded.

My back was aching and my side was throbbing and my arms were burning but I hardly noticed any of it.

I was too busy noticing the look on Gran's face.

I know you made her come and rescue me, Doug, and I'm really grateful.

But seeing her peering at me like that, her face all pink and concerned, I had the weird thought that even if you hadn't made her rush out with that bucket of water, she probably would have anyway.

Mum went gastric.

'Oh Jeez!' she yelled. 'Ring Doctor Masterton.'

Mum, I thought, stop over-reacting.

Then I remembered that as well as being dripping wet and covered in dust and a bit scraped around the chin, I still had blood on my nose and a swollen knee from the gym mats.

'It's OK, Mum,' I said, 'it'll wash off.'

Sonya Masterton reckons her dad's workload has doubled since the bank started chucking people off their farms and I didn't want him taking it out on me with tetanus injections.

'Where's that hopeless husband of yours?' said Gran to Mum, grabbing me by the shoulder. 'I want him to take a squiz at this. See what his precious bank's doing.'

My side started throbbing harder.

'No,' said Mum. 'Noel's had enough today. Head office just rang. Mr Grimmond reckons Noel's reports are too soft. Told him he's making too many excuses for the farmers. Told him to get tougher or else. He's taken a Panadol and gone to bed.'

Poor old Dad.

He's probably feeling as bad as I am.

I'm in the bath now, checking out the damage.

Few bruises mostly.

Nothing that'll get in the way of diving practice.

What I need is some softer gym mats.

Gran's just been in.

I wish she'd knock.

She might be good at handling bullies but she's got hopeless manners when it comes to bathrooms.

She told me to run more water and soak my bruises properly, but I didn't cause we're getting low and the next delivery's not for ages.

Plus she's already used a bucketful out in the street.

'Thanks, Gran,' I said. 'You really put the wind up the Malleys.'

Gran waved a letter at me.

'I wouldn't have done it,' she said, 'if I'd known you'd been stealing my mail.'

I stared up at her.

'It was in your school bag,' she said. 'Dunno how a person's meant to manage their investments when letters from their bank get left in school bags.'

I realised what had happened.

This morning, when I was at the mail box checking for birthday cards and I panicked about Dad and the Malleys, I must have stuffed her letter in my bag.

'Sorry, Gran,' I said.

She grunted.

I saw her looking at my bruises and I could tell she was blaming Dad.

'It was my fault,' I said. 'I wanted to fight the Malleys and get it out the way so I can concentrate on being a champion diver.'

She stared down at me.

'I knew I wouldn't get too bashed,' I said, 'cause Doug's back looking after me.'

Gran's stare turned into a frown.

I hope I didn't hurt her feelings, letting her know she didn't save me single-handed.

I hope she was just frowning cause Grandad's been dead seven years and it's a long time since she's seen a willy.

Chapter Twelve

G'day Doug.

If you've got a sec, I'll explain what I'm doing up here on the roof.

And what all the mattresses and pillows and cushions from the house are doing piled up down there on the ground.

It's like this.

Last night before I went to sleep I decided to get a bit of diving practice in.

Mr Tristos is always saying that to learn something new you've got to do it several times.

Trouble is, it's really hard doing a double somersault off the top of a wardrobe onto a bed.

The most I could do was a single somersault with a half twist.

I hadn't even planned the half twist, I had to do it to avoid the bedside lamp.

For a double somersault you need extra height, so now Mum and Dad have left early for work, I've decided to use our roof.

The reason I'm telling you all this, Doug, is I'm a bit worried that if I bounce off the mattresses at the wrong angle there might not be enough pillows and cushions to stop me splitting my skull open and scattering teeth all over the driveway.

I don't want to wake Gran up to ask her for her pillow, so I'm asking you to keep an eye on me.

Thanks, Doug.

OK, I'd better stop yakking and get a few dives in before my soles melt and stick to the roof.

I don't want to be up here scraping my thongs off the tin when Gran wakes up.

If Mum and Dad find out about this they'll go mental.

Mum and Dad have gone mental.

I've tried to explain to them it's partly their fault for coming home only ten minutes after they left.

They should have told me they were just going to Conkey's for tights and aftershave.

But they won't listen.

They're too busy yelling things up at me like 'don't move' and 'step back off the guttering' and 'I'm gunna tan your hide' and 'don't jump, we love you'.

I'm trying to tell them about my diving

career and how I was never in serious danger and neither were the lounge room cushions because you were protecting me, Doug.

I know they don't believe in you, but I don't know what else to say.

I've got to calm them down somehow.

Oh, no.

Dad's climbing up the ladder.

Help him, Doug, please.

No, it's OK, I can handle it.

Once I've unhooked his trouser leg from the TV satellite dish and unjammed his shoe from the bathroom window, he'll be fine.

Doug, are you feeling hurt?

You know, by the things Mum and Dad have just been saying about you?

They weren't really about you.

When Dad said 'Oh God, not again', it was mostly because when I got him off the ladder he was so tense he sat on the four-wheel drive winch and ripped his daks for the second time this week.

When Mum said 'Mitch, I thought we agreed three years ago you were too old for all this invisible friend nonsense', she only used the word nonsense because she was tired and stressed and wondering how she could get two windows fixed before work.

When Dad said to Mum 'It's all your

mother's fault for filling his head with loony hairbrained gibberish in the first place', he was just letting off steam because of the unkind things Gran says to him, and possibly because the winch had irritated his upper thighs.

I hope that makes you feel better, Doug.

Now we're all sitting at the breakfast table and there's some silence at last, I'm gunna try and work it out.

The thing that's puzzling me.

Doug, why didn't you delay Mum and Dad a bit?

To give me time to get at least one dive in?

After they left Conkey's you could have made them drop into the Gas 'N' Gobble for some touch-up paint to cover the rude words people have scratched on the side of Dad's four-wheel drive.

You could have inspired them to come home via the scenic route past the abattoir.

Why didn't you, Doug?

Was it cause you're angry with me for having parents who don't believe in you?

Hang on a sec, Mum's just started to cry.

'You could have been killed,' she's saying.

Poor thing.

I feel terrible.

I wish I could make her feel better.

All I can do is hug her.

'For God's sake speak to him,' she's saying to Dad.

We're all waiting.

Dad looks pretty upset too.

'You could have been killed,' he's saying.

He's just knocked the milk over.

'Hopeless,' Gran's saying.

Everyone's silent again.

I reckon I know the answer, Doug.

I reckon you're not angry.

Mum and Dad can't help what they believe, you know that.

I reckon you stopped me diving this morning for their sake.

In a town this small, they'd find out sooner or later about me diving onto gym mats and lounge cushions, and the stress would be too much.

Look at poor old Dad.

He's so stressed he's just shut his tie in the fridge.

Now he's glaring at the fridge door like he's planning to write a report on it.

OK, Doug, I get the message.

From now on I'll only dive into water.

I just wish the excursion was tomorrow instead of next week.

When the bus gets to the coast, I'm gunna spend half a minute having a squiz at the sea, just to check out what it looks like, then

I'll go straight to the pool and start practising.

Doug, please make Dad's heart valves stand the stress until the excursion.

Chapter Thirteen

The excursion's been cancelled.

Ms Dorrit just told us in assembly.

Kids are almost in tears.

Me included.

Leaving the hall we were all numb, just sort of staring at the ground.

Well, I was staring at the ground.

The others were staring at me and muttering how it was all my fault.

Luckily I didn't have to go into class with them. Ms Dorrit sent me to stand here outside her door after what she reckoned was my outburst in assembly.

I reckon an outburst's only human with news that bad.

What got me was she didn't even look sad.

When a school principal stands up in assembly and comes out with news that crook, you'd think she'd at least look sad, eh Doug?

'I've got some very disappointing news,' she said after we'd finished singing.

I reckon she's not disappointed at all.

I reckon she's glad.

I reckon she never liked the idea of a school excursion in case Cathy Saxby chucked on the bus.

'Regretfully,' she said, 'we haven't had enough bookings for the excursion and I have no alternative but to cancel it.'

My insides did a dive.

No somersaults.

No twists.

Just a straight plummet.

I looked around.

I've never seen a hallful of kids so sad.

Most of the kids in this town can't even swim and that trip to the coast was their only chance to learn.

I could see what they were thinking.

Andy Howard was thinking that if he ever visits a Mexican food factory and falls into a vat of taco dip and finds he can't eat it fast enough, he'll drown.

Sheena Bullock was thinking that if she and her dog join the police force and chase smugglers and her dog gets hit on the head with a surfboard stuffed with jewels, she'll never be able to swim over and rescue him.

Danielle Wicks was thinking that when she becomes Prime Minister, if she falls into that lake in Canberra she'll be history.

Carla Fiami was looking sadder than any of them.

I reckon she was thinking about her childhood growing up on the coast and how she'll probably never get to have another swim ever again.

I knew what they were all thinking because I was thinking about my future life too.

Not a life of international sporting glory and having my picture taken with Dad for the bowls club newsletter.

A life of being hounded from town to town and only being spoken to by the kids of dentists and parking inspectors.

A life of brooding how close I'd come to saving my family.

And how I'd failed.

I looked up at Ms Dorrit on the stage.

'You can't,' I said.

She looked stunned, then glared down at me.

My mouth was dryer than a lawn sprinkler.

'You can't cancel the excursion,' I croaked. 'Do you have any idea what it's like to drown in taco dip?'

It was a pretty dumb thing to say, but it didn't matter because Ms Dorrit ignored it.

'I didn't choose this, Mitch Webber,' she said. 'It breaks my heart too.'

I didn't know I was gunna say the next thing till I'd said it.

73

'Bull,' I said to Ms Dorrit. 'If you really cared you'd get our pool here in town filled so the kids and dogs of this district could learn to swim and we could have our own swimming carnival.'

Ms Dorrit's eyes narrowed.

'And diving competition,' I said.

She opened her mouth.

For a sec I thought she was gunna say, 'Good idea Mitch, I'll order the water today.'

Instead she just pointed to her room.

As I walked out, she turned back to the assembly.

'It's not my choice,' she said. 'I've been contacted by many of your parents. They've told me they just don't have the money for an excursion, not with the drought on, not with all their other financial problems.'

As soon as she said that, every kid in the hall stopped looking at her and turned and looked at me.

Not just looked at me, glared at me.

Suddenly I couldn't breathe.

All around me, eyes were ripping into me like bullets.

Not just Troy and Brent Malley's, everyone's.

I've never seen a hallful of kids looking so mean.

If they'd had cattle trucks they'd have driven them over me there and then.

My guts did a slow belly flop as I realised what they were thinking.

I opened my mouth to try and explain, then gave it away.

I knew they'd still be thinking what they were thinking even if I explained for hours.

Even if I yelled till I was blue in the face.

The excursion's off, they were thinking, because of Mitch Webber's dad.

Oh well, thanks for making Ms Dorrit not expel me, Doug.

I know you couldn't do anything about the excursion.

An angel's job is to protect people, not fix up their travel arrangements or fill up their swimming pools.

Some problems can only be solved by us people ourselves.

That's why instead of going back to class I'm squeezing through this hole in the school fence.

Chapter Fourteen

Mayors should be more polite and considerate, that's what I reckon.

If a person comes into their video store for a meeting, they should turn the volume down on their TV.

How can anyone be expected to discuss serious council business with *The Little Mermaid* blaring in the background?

Mr Bullock couldn't even hear what I was saying at first.

'The swimming pool,' I shouted.

He turned the video down.

'I reckon,' I went on, 'if that pool was filled it could save this town. Truckies would stop off for a dip and spend money at the kiosk and tourists would come and pay fees at the camp-ground and the local economy would boom and the bank wouldn't have to chuck families off their properties and who knows, someone from round here could become an international diving champion and really put this town on the map.'

Mayors ought to be more dignified, too.

When someone suggests something really important to them they ought to look serious and say 'I'll make sure the council gives it their fullest consideration next time we're having a drink at the bowls club'.

Not laugh out loud and stick their hand down their shorts for a scratch.

When I'm world diving champ and I come home to accept the keys of the town, no way am I accepting them from him.

Anyway, he's wrong.

I'm absolutly positive that if the council bought half a million litres of water for the pool, people would not think it was the same as the councillors sticking the money in their bottoms, setting fire to it and doing cartwheels around town.

Mr Bullock's also wrong about the state of the pool.

I'm checking it out now and it's nowhere near as bad as he says.

OK, the fence is very rusty, but that's only a problem when you're climbing over it in a white T-shirt like I just did.

The turnstiles are pretty rusty too, but

they'll soon loosen up once kids start pushing them with blockout on their hands.

And the steps up to the diving board have seen better days, but people aren't idiots, they're capable of looking out for a few loose bits of concrete and a wobbly handrail.

Down here inside the pool itself things aren't too bad at all.

The paint on the bottom and sides is peeling a bit, but you've got to expect that when it's been dry as a duck's dunny for eight years.

The important thing is there are no big cracks, so it won't leak.

When these soft drink cans and chip wrappers and old shotgun cartridges are cleaned out it'll be good as new.

Once I've got it filled up.

Which won't be easy.

Gran always reckons when you've got a problem, make a list of all the things you could do to solve it, even the dopey ones.

Here goes.

I could ring the city and pretend to be the Gas 'N' Gobble and order two million cans of Coke and use them to fill the pool. Trouble is parents'd be dragging their kids out every five minutes to make them clean their teeth.

I could stick lots of hoses together and syphon the beer out of the bowls club. But then only people over eighteen would be allowed in the pool.

I could persuade everyone in town to come down here on a really hot day and sweat a lot. If I lived in a town with more people.

No Doug, it'll have to be water.

It'll be pretty hard getting hold of half a million litres of the stuff, but it's the only way.

It'll be pretty risky, too.

Not just for me, for the other kids as well.

Some of them might need an eye kept out for them.

I'll do the best I can Doug, but I might need some help, OK?

Chapter Fifteen

For a while it looked as if the meeting was going to be as big a disaster as my birthday party, even though I tried even harder this time.

I made the invitation sound as important as I could.

VERY IMPORTANT MEETING, I wrote. THIS MEETING COULD SAVE YOUR LIFE. IF YOU EVER PLAN TO VISIT A NON-DROUGHT AREA (EG CANBERRA, THE COAST OR A TACO DIP FACTORY), BE AT THIS MEETING. AFTER SCHOOL AT THE DUMP. NO PARENTS OR DOBBERS.

I stuck an invitation in every school locker like last time, but this time I included a map. Even though it wasn't really needed cause everyone in town goes to the dump at least once a week with their garbage, twice if they're looking for fridge parts.

When I got to the dump it was deserted.

Except, for a sec, I thought you were there Doug.

A breeze was making the plastic bags flap and was pinging the dust against the old tractor parts.

Then I remembered how Mr Conkey once explained that air movement at the dump is caused by gas from rotting potato peel. (At the time he was trying to get everyone to buy frozen potato wedges.)

I waited by the piles of plastic drink bottles we collected last year when the council went on a recycling craze. We saved bottles for months, right up until someone remembered the nearest recycling plant is two thousand kilometres away.

By ten past three only two kids had arrived and they ignored me and started chucking Mrs Nile's bedsprings at each other.

By three-fifteen I was desperate.

I started wondering if a diving competition could be held in real life with just wardrobes and beds.

Then I saw a bunch of about twenty kids coming towards me.

As they got closer, looking hot and annoyed, I saw Carla Fiami behind them, yapping at the stragglers' heels like a cattle dog.

'You'll never know if he's crapping on or not if you don't give him a listen,' I heard her saying to Troy and Brent Malley. 'Give him

81

five minutes and if you still reckon he's a slimebucket, bash him up then.'

Carla grinned at me and I gave her a grateful look, but not too grateful.

The kids gathered round and I climbed up onto Mr Saxby's old ute and tried to ignore Troy and Brent's noisy breathing.

'I've worked out a way,' I said as loudly as I could, which wasn't very loud cause my throat was dryer than a lawn sprinkler, 'of getting the pool filled.'

The kids stared at me.

The dump was silent except for the flapping plastic and the pinging dust and the sound of Emma Wilkinson getting her foot jammed in a paint tin.

'Bull,' said Troy Malley after a bit.

'You're gunna ask my uncle, right?' said Hazel Gillies. 'His tribe can get water out of rocks with wallaby guts. He'll fill the pool for youse. Next year when he gets back from Perth.'

I thanked Hazel for her offer and pointed across the dump at the reservoir tower in the distance.

'There's enough water in there to fill the pool,' I said. 'More than enough. Six hundred thousand litres.'

The kids stared at me even harder.

Carla was starting to look worried.

Troy and Brent Malley were starting to look impatient and angry.

'You can't use that,' said Matthew Conn. 'That's the town's water supply. That's got to last till the next delivery.'

'If you use that,' said Danielle Wicks, 'what are we meant to wash in?'

'What are we meant to drink?' said Sean Howe.

'What are we meant to boil two-minute noodles in?' said Andy Howard.

'The people round here need that water,' said Jacquie Chaplin.

'That's why,' I said, 'we're gunna let them use it first.'

During the silence that followed I jumped down from the ute and grabbed an armful of empty plastic drink bottles and started handing them round.

Most of the kids looked puzzled, specially Troy and Brent Malley.

Carla Fiami grinned.

Three bottles.

Not bad for one evening.

It would have been more if Mum had boiled something for dinner instead of microwaving, and if I'd been a bit quicker with the sponge when Dad dropped the kettle.

Tomorrow after school I'll get a proper plug for the shower.

I don't know if you've ever tried to save your shower water, Doug, but you're fighting a losing battle when the plug's made of toilet paper and keeps going soggy.

Come to think of it, angels probably don't need showers. You probably just fly so fast all the dirt gets blown off.

Thanks for keeping Gran out of the bathroom while I was getting the shower water into the bottles.

Best if the adults don't know about the plan yet.

If they knew there was a secret stash of water in town, they'd probably all want to wash their cars.

I think the plan's gunna work, Doug.

I just saw Carla in the playground and she's got six bottles already.

Six bottles in less than a day.

She explained that only two are from her place cause they've got a special shower spray that hardly lets any water through, plus she got shampoo in her eyes this morning and kicked the plug out and lost about another two bottles.

The other four bottles are from the Gas 'N' Gobble.

Carla had to meet her mum there yesterday after the meeting and Geoff the mechanic was flushing out a ute radiator and she asked if she could have the water.

She said it was for a project, which is almost true.

Pretty smart thinking, eh Doug?

Water's water, even if it is a bit rusty.

If all the kids are as on the ball as Carla, we'll have the pool filled in no time.

OK, not all the kids are as on the ball as Carla.

Just now going into class Danielle Wicks saw me and tried to walk the other way so I cornered her.

She showed me what she'd collected.

Half a bottle.

Half a bottle from a family of seven.

'What about all the people having showers at your place?' I asked.

'We don't get showers on Thursdays,' said Danielle, 'just a bath with all of us using the same water.'

I looked at her half bottle in amazement.

'Seven of you have a bath in that much water?' I said.

'Don't be a pin brain,' she said. 'We use heaps more than that but Ryan goes last and he lets the dogs drink it.'

I asked her to keep her voice down. We

were pretty close to the offices and Ms Dorrit's got ears like a council irrigation inspector.

Quietly I suggested to Danielle that the more she can stop their dogs running around and getting thirsty, the quicker we'll have the pool filled.

She scowled.

'Listen, smarty pants,' she said, 'don't get bossy just cause you can pinch crates of bank water. Your dad and his poxy bank are the reason our family's living in a poxy house in town in the first place with three dogs going mental in the yard.'

I decided not to get into an argument.

Life must be pretty tough for the Wicks's, plus when Danielle gets worked up her voice can be heard for miles.

I started to quietly explain to her that the bank doesn't supply its staff with water, just tea and coffee.

Danielle unscrewed her bottle and tried to tip it over my head.

With another 499,986 litres still to get we can't afford to waste water, so I shut up.

Most of the kids are trying to avoid me.

Andy Howard reckons trying to fill the pool is a dopey idea and that his mum's pot plants need the water more cause if her cherry tomatoes die she'll kill him.

~

Matthew Conn hasn't collected a drop.

He says his dad goes really crook if anyone in his family has a shower or washes clothes and doesn't use the water to top up the radiator in the truck.

I just bailed up Sean Howe in the boys' dunny.

He hasn't collected a drop either.

He reckons he doesn't dare cause his mum and dad use all their cooking water for making beer.

He offered to pee into a bottle, but I said no.

You'd think, wouldn't you Doug, that a townful of fairly intelligent kids could do a simple thing like save household water.

Jeez.

I can see why Mr Tristos gets so stressed when he has to try and organise everyone for sport. If I had a moustache like Mr Tristos I'd be chewing it right now, I can tell you.

I've just wasted three hours after school waiting for kids to turn up with some water.

OK, the time wasn't completely wasted. The first hour I spent clearing rubbish out of the pool changing rooms so we've got somewhere to stack the full bottles.

The next hour I spent finding the Stegnjaaics' old inflatable plastic swimming pool at the dump and dragging empty bottles back in it and hiding them in the pool kiosk.

But the last hour I just waited.

And did some thinking.

I reckon I know now what the problem is, Doug.

None of those kids believe in you.

None of them believe you can save them from being sprung by their parents and whacked round the head with wilting pot plants and dried-up home-brewing kits.

There must be something we can do to change that.

Chapter Sixteen

Sorry to disturb you so late, Doug, but I've thought of something.

I'm not sure if you're going to like it.

Or even if it's possible.

Oh well, here goes.

What I'm hoping, Doug, is that angels can stop being invisible for a bit and appear to kids.

You know, if there's a really really important reason for them to do it, like saving a town and a dad.

I've been thinking about it for hours since I went to bed and I reckon it is possible.

I read in the paper once about some kids in Peru who said they saw an angel, and I reckon they were telling the truth. I reckon Dad was wrong about them having fried their brains from sitting too close to their computer screens.

If their angel could appear to them, I reckon you could appear to a group of kids in this town standing on your head.

Not actually standing on your head but, though you can if you want.

In a blaze of light would be better.

With fireworks in the background.

And maybe some laser beams or something.

If I arrange things this end, could you do it tomorrow night?

Please?

It's all set, Doug.

Wasn't easy, but.

None of the kids believed me at first.

'Bull,' said Matthew Conn.

'As if,' said Jacquie Chaplin.

'Jeez, you're a pin brain,' said Danielle Wicks.

'It's true,' I said.

'Yeah, right,' sneered Andy Howard. 'What's this angel gunna do after he's appeared, drop into the Gas 'N' Gobble for some hot chips and a grease and oil change on his wings?'

The others all laughed, which just shows how desperate kids in this town are for real entertainment.

I frantically tried to think of something to take their minds off being pikers.

'It'll be pretty spectacular,' I said. 'Fireworks, probably.'

'I doubt it,' said Cathy Saxby. 'Seeing as there's been a total fire ban for the last eight years.'

'Pin brain,' said Danielle Wicks.

They started to wander off.

I was losing them.

Then Carla saved me.

'If Doug does show up,' she said, 'where's he gunna show up at?'

Her eyes were glittering and I couldn't tell if she was having a go at me or not.

Out of the corner of my eye I saw Troy and Brent Malley walking towards me across the playground with mean faces and that was when I had the idea.

'The Malleys' place,' I said loudly. 'Doug's gunna appear tonight down by the creek bed at the Malleys' place.'

The other kids stopped and turned and looked at Troy and Brent.

My mouth was dryer than a garden tap, but I made it keep on talking.

'And when the world hears about it,' I said to Troy and Brent, 'your place'll probably become a top tourist attraction and you won't have to move.'

Troy and Brent looked at each other.

Then they looked at me.

'Fair dinkum?' said Troy.

'Yes,' I said.

The other kids looked at me and then at Troy and Brent again and then at me again.

Brent put his face close to mine.

'If you're bulling, we'll do you,' he said.
'I know,' I said.
'What time?' asked Sean Howe.
I told them about eight.
Hope that's OK with you, Doug.

We're all here, Doug, and the other kids are getting a bit restless.

Troy and Brent reckon if you don't appear in the next minute they're gunna stab me.

It's too dark to see if they've got knives, but even if they haven't there's heaps of other things they could use out here in the scrub. Dry spinifex, for example. They'll find sharp bits easily, specially now the other kids are offering to help them look.

Carla's trying to calm them down.

She's telling them to go easy on me because I'm not a bad person, I'm just a bit of an idiot.

Sometimes I wish she wouldn't help quite so much.

I've already told them you're a bit late cause you're probably trying to decide what to wear.

Anything'll do, Doug.

Robes, a loincloth, overalls, anything.

And if the fireworks and lasers are holding things up, forget about them.

I've got a torch.

I did have a torch.

Troy and Brent have just taken it.

I think they're looking for a snake.

I think they're muttering something about my pants.

I can't hear exactly cause the other kids are sniggering too loudly.

Hurry, Doug, please.

Yes.

At last.

You're here.

Thank you.

The others have seen you too.

That's a great idea Doug, just having two beams of light instead of anything too flashy.

They look a bit like headlights coming towards us.

They are headlights.

Jeez, you're clever Doug.

Other angels would have floated down on a shimmering cloud with blinding special effects going off all over the place, but you've turned up in an ordinary old four-wheel drive so as not to scare anyone.

I can't believe it, Doug.

I've waited so long to meet you.

I'm so happy.

The tears are just cause your headlights are dazzling me a bit.

I'm over here.

The one waving.

You're waving too, I can see you now.

Leaning out of the driver's window.

Yelling.

Oh no, you're angry.

I must have dragged you away from something important.

Doug, I'm sorry, but now you're here you'll see that this is important too.

Look, the kids are all gawping.

Now they can see you with their own eyes they know they're being looked after by a real live top-quality guardian angel who'll keep them safe in even the riskiest water-bottling situations and . . .

Hang on a sec, Doug.

That's not you.

I know that voice.

I know that face.

Chapter Seventeen

I don't get it, Doug.

OK, I know you not turning up tonight must have been because you were flat out.

Guiding a school bus through a burning carwash, something like that.

And I know that not being able to answer my call would have probably made you feel pretty crook.

So sending someone else would have seemed like a good idea at the time.

But, Doug, why Dad?

I guess even angels don't always think straight when they're in the middle of a major rescue with blazing hoses and melting plastic buckets all around them.

If you'd had a moment to gather your thoughts you'd have realised that almost anyone would have been a better choice.

Mum.

Gran.

Mr Bullock with burning banknotes sticking out of his bum.

Anyone but Dad.

I've told you heaps of times how clumsy Dad gets when he's stressed.

One of the things that stresses him most is me being out in the bush at night.

He's got this thing about it ever since Marija Stegnjaaic got bitten by a scorpion at night and her tongue turned black.

This evening when Dad turned up at the Malleys' place he was so stressed he couldn't even drive properly.

He was crunching the gears so much he sounded like Gran eating chocolate crackles. That's why I thought it was you at first, Doug. Angels probably don't get much practice driving four-wheel drives.

The other kids weren't fooled.

They did stare at the four-wheel drive with their mouths open, but only after Dad had driven into a tree.

'Mitch,' he yelled after he'd checked for dents. 'Get in the vehicle.'

'That's not an angel,' said Sean Howe. 'That's your dad.'

'You're mental, Mitch Webber,' hissed Cathy Saxby. 'You should be living in sheltered accommodation.'

I got into the car, but only because I could

see Troy and Brent in the headlights running over to the house to tell Mr and Mrs Malley about their only tree.

Dad glared at me, then stuck his head out the window again.

'The rest of you stay here,' he yelled to the others. 'Your parents are on the way.'

The other kids looked at each other, then glared at me.

I couldn't hear what they were saying because Dad was revving the engine so much.

I didn't need to.

I'm getting pretty good at lip-reading swear words.

The four-wheel drive shot backwards.

And stopped.

Dad revved the engine even more.

'You can thank your lucky stars,' he shouted at me while he did it, 'that Ryan Wicks spilled the beans to his folks about tonight's little fiasco.'

Doug, I reckon that's really low.

Was that the only way you could get Dad out to the Malleys' tonight, by using a little kid like Ryan?

When Danielle finds out he dobbed, she'll kill him.

It was low, but not as low as what happened when Dad finally stopped revving the engine and found we were bogged in sand.

'Give us a push,' he yelled to the other kids. 'Please.'

None of them moved.

And when their parents arrived, none of them helped either.

They just looked at me and Dad stuffing sticks under the wheels and turned away.

Some even sniggered.

Even Carla didn't help, but that was probably because she was depending on Danielle Wicks' parents for a lift and she didn't want to offend them.

'I tried to tell you,' she said as she walked past. 'Only dopes believe in guardian angels.'

She had to say that cause Danielle was with her.

Me and Dad were there for hours.

Mr and Mrs Malley threatened to have us arrested for trespassing and soil erosion.

Finally we got unbogged.

'That Fiami girl, she's right about guardian angels,' was all Dad said on the way home.

I didn't say anything.

Carla's right about a lot of stuff but she's not right about that.

She's not, is she Doug?

Chapter Eighteen

I can't sleep.

My eyes keep watering.

I've been telling myself it's the sand in my undies pricking me, but it's not.

It's what happened tonight.

First at the Malleys' and then just now.

I heard Gran get up and go out to the kitchen so I got up too and went out for a chat.

'Want a chocolate crackle?' asked Gran.

She gets pains in her legs at night and chocolate helps.

I shook my head.

'Gran,' I said, 'am I too old to have a guardian angel?'

Gran looked at me and took a big puff of her cigarette.

I felt myself flinch, and it wasn't because I was scared she'd cough chocolate crackle over me.

It was because I was scared of what her answer would be.

She blew the smoke out and then did something she hasn't done for ages.

Came over and gave me a hug.

'Jeez Mitch,' she said quietly, 'if I'd known it was gunna go on this long I'd never have started it.'

I pulled away from her.

'What do you mean?' I said.

My chest felt all tight, and it wasn't because I'd strained it pushing the car.

Gran took another mouthful and another puff.

'When I told you that story about Doug,' she said, 'you weren't even knee-high to a tick.'

My chest suddenly felt like a water bag when people are squeezing it to get the last drops out.

'Story,' I said. 'What story?'

'You'd wake up bawling,' said Gran. 'When it rained. Used to do that in those days. You were only three and a bit but you had galvanised-iron lungs. Your mum was tuckered out and your dad was hopeless, so I used to come over and tell you a story. About Doug, your guardian angel.'

She reached over and gripped my arm.

Her fingers were really strong for a senior citizen.

'Mitch,' she said quietly, 'mate, it was just a story.'

I stared at her and waited for my mouth to stop twitching.

So I could tell her that she'd got it wrong.

That you're not a story, Doug, you're true.

She'd said so herself.

Night after night.

I clenched my teeth and pointed this out to her and started reminding her of some stuff.

How you saved me from the Malleys.

Twice.

Then I realised she couldn't hear a word over the coughing fit she was having.

I slapped her on the back and poured her a beer and I was just about to start again when Mum came in with half-open eyes moaning about the racket and sent us both back to bed.

'If you wake Dad,' she growled at me, 'after what you put him through earlier tonight, you're dingo bait.'

'Sorry,' I mumbled.

Gran grabbed me outside my room.

For a sec, Doug, I thought she was going to tell me she'd been pulling my leg and that you were as real as the yellow stains on her fingers.

She didn't.

She just gave me another hug, which was sweet of her even though it nearly dislocated my ear.

'We don't need angels, old mate,' she said. 'We can look after each other, eh?'

I looked at her crumpled ancient face and realised what's happened.

It's tragic, eh Doug, when old people start to lose their grip.

I should have spotted it earlier.

Gran's been putting her lipstick on wobbly for some time now.

Jeez, she gave me a scare, but.

Imagine if you were really just someone she'd made up?

If you didn't exist?

I'd be on my own.

Just me and dog poo for my birthday and a dad people won't help even when he's up to his axles.

Just thinking about it's making my eyes go drippy.

I hate it when brains do this.

Get flooded with scary thoughts late at night.

It's OK, Doug.

I know you do really exist.

That's why I'm just sniffling a bit.

If I was really on my own I'd be sobbing much harder than this.

My tears'd probably fill the town pool.

Chapter Nineteen

Yes!
    Yes!
    Yes!
    Yes!
    Yes!
    Go Doug!
    Yes!!!!!

I deserve to be tied down in the scrub with jam on my big toes and heaps of signposts so the ants can find me.

No, Doug, I do.

It's what I deserve.

For not having more faith in you.

For doubting the double-best guardian angel in the whole universe.

Give us a D!

Give us an O!

Give us a U!

Give us a G!

What does it spell?

GENIUS!

I dunno how you did it, Doug, but thanks.

If God ever retires, I reckon you should get the job, no argument.

When the shouting woke me up my heart nearly dived out of my chest.

We don't usually get big crowds in town that early on a Saturday, so for an awful sec I thought it was farmers with guns coming after Dad.

I think Dad did too.

When I came out of my room he was crouched behind the kitchen table.

Though that might just have been because he'd stubbed his toe on the fridge again.

'Don't worry, Dad,' I said, 'I'll check it out.'

I peered out the front door ready to duck bullets.

Then I realised the shouting wasn't angry and murderous, it was happy and excited.

When I got down to the main street, half the town was milling around.

There were plenty of farmers, and I could tell they'd just driven in fast because their dogs were still in the back of their utes. A dog won't go onto a bonnet till the engine's cooled a bit.

The farmers weren't loading guns and muttering things about Dad, they were yelling questions at each other and pointing out along the highway.

For a sec I thought it was you, Doug.

Making your appearance a bit late and in slightly the wrong place.

Which would have been fine.

Even geniuses with super powers beyond the reach of mere mortals can't be expected to read maps right every time.

When the cloud of dust everyone was pointing at got a bit closer and I saw it wasn't you, I wasn't too disappointed.

Not when I saw what it was.

'Jeez,' yelled a farmer next to me, 'look at the size of them.'

Actually, as road tankers go, I don't reckon they were that much bigger than the one that brings petrol to the Gas 'N' Gobble on the first Wednesday of each month.

They were shinier, that's all.

And they didn't have Shell written on the side.

Or black smears all over them like the one that delivers the council water. The one that everybody reckons used to carry road tar.

People just thought your tankers were bigger, Doug, because they were so gleaming and mysterious.

And there were three of them.

We don't get many mysteries in these parts.

Not ones that don't involve banks or governments.

That's why everyone ran along the main street next to your tankers yelling and hollering even before they knew where the tankers were going.

I knew where they were going.

That's why I yelled and hollered louder than anyone.

Because I was so happy.

When the tankers stopped at the pool and the first one backed up to the gate and the driver connected a huge hose to the rear, everyone else got pretty happy too.

Except Mr Bullock.

He must be the most depressed mayor in Australia, I reckon.

'You can't fill this pool without council permission,' he said to the driver.

The driver hesitated.

The rest of us ignored him and jumped into the pool and started clearing out the rubbish.

Mr Bullock knew he was beaten.

'Alright,' he said, 'but the council's not paying for this water.'

'It's taken care of,' said the driver.

For a heart-stopping sec I thought he was you, Doug.

He didn't have wings, but if crumb-trays on

toasters can be detachable, I don't see why wings can't be too.

Then Matthew Conn tried to turn the big tap at the back of the tanker and the driver gave him a slap on the head.

So I knew it wasn't you, Doug, cause you'd never hit a kid.

When the driver turned the tap and the jet of water hit the wall of the pool, I held my breath in case the tired old concrete exploded.

It didn't.

All that exploded was the loudest cheer I've ever heard in this town, including the day we got satellite TV and Mr Conkey sold Mars Bars at half price.

Mr Bullock had one last try for the title of Australia's Grumpiest Mayor.

'No swimming,' he yelled at a couple of kids who were about to jump in. 'Council health regulations. No swimming without pool chemicals in the water. It's unsanitary.'

When the drivers opened the storage compartments under the tankers and started dragging out the drums of pool chlorine, the cheer that went up was almost as loud as the first one.

Would have been louder, probably, if some of the farmers hadn't been using their energy to chuck Mr Bullock into the pool.

Thanks, Doug.

I'd hug you if I could.

I'm hugging my wardrobe and pretending it's you.

When I'm a champion diver I'll mention you in all my interviews.

Plus, when the pool opens for swimming this afternoon, I'm gunna tell everyone who provided the water.

They'll want to name the pool after you, no risk.

Have angels got second names?

Don't worry if you haven't, Doug.

You can use mine.

Chapter Twenty

I hope you can see this, Doug.

The view from up here on this diving board is incredible.

I can see the whole town, and the abattoir, and the Gas 'N' Gobble who need to repaint their roof pretty soon, and every property Dad's ever dobbed on.

Well, almost every property.

I can't actually tell them apart cause they all look the same from up here.

Brown.

Sorry Doug, I'm forgetting you'd be used to panoramic views.

So I don't have to tell you how much smaller a swimming pool seems when you're looking down on it.

Specially when half the town's in it trying to learn how to swim.

There hasn't been this much splashing in these parts since Danielle Wicks' mum tried to wash six dogs in the one bath.

Nobody's drowned yet, so swimming can't be that hard.

I reckon once I'm in the water I'll grasp the basics pretty quickly.

With a bit of help from you, Doug.

I had lots of Rice Bubbles for breakfast, so at least I'll float.

That was a good thought, Doug, only half-filling the pool.

Sergeant Crean reckons the water's too shallow for diving into from up here, which has stopped everyone else from having a crack at being a world-champion diver.

Boy, it's a long way down.

It's OK, Doug, I'm not scared.

This isn't me trembling, it's just me shivering a bit in the breeze. We're not used to breezes around here.

Plus my blood's pounding a bit.

From excitement.

My first real dive.

I can't wait.

Well actually I can wait cause if I dive now I'll land on Mr Saxby.

And Mrs Saxby who's holding his neck brace while he practises butterfly.

And Gavin Sims who keeps sinking to the bottom cause he's using his dad's cricket bat as a kick-board.

And Jacquie Chaplin who can feel something uncomfortable in her swimmers.

And Hazel Gillies who's telling her it's Gavin's foot.

And ...

I know, Doug, I know.

I've got to wait for a patch of water and go for it.

It's the same as waiting for the right moment to tell everyone why they should put up a big sign saying DOUG WEBBER SWIMMING POOL.

While I'm waiting I'll just focus my mind.

That's the most important thing for a diver, focussing the mind.

All the telly commentators say so.

First I think arms.

Now I think legs.

Now I think what if Mr Saxby has a neck spasm and flops into my patch of water while I'm on my way down.

Now I think stop being such a worry wart.

Now I think Doug wouldn't let it happen.

Now I think he's already done something today that proves he's the most super-powerful and clever angel in the entire known stratosphere i.e. half-filled a pool in thirteen minutes without using a single plastic bottle.

Now I think if he can do that he can do anything.

Move mountains.

Move tired sheep.

End droughts.

Stop me flattening Mr Saxby or any member of his . . .

Hang on a sec.

Jeez.

Doug.

I'm so slow.

Of course.

You could.

After this morning I know you could.

Now I am trembling.

And not just cause Sergeant Crean's climbing up and yelling at me that the diving board's a prohibited area.

Don't worry about him, Doug.

Don't waste time giving him vertigo or leg cramps.

Listen to what I'm saying.

I'm going to ask you the most important thing I've ever asked you.

Ever.

Including when I begged you to save me from that killer spider in first year.

Doug, I'm asking you to end the drought.

Make it rain, Doug.

You can do it, I know.

It's just like what you did today only with more water.

Doug, ignore Sergeant Crean even though he is grabbing me a bit roughly.

Focus your mind, Doug.

End the drought.

Please.

Chapter Twenty-one

Doug?

Are you there?

Ignore me if you've started focussing your mind on ending the drought, OK?

I know it's a huge job and the last thing you want is me yakking away at you. That's why I haven't been in touch for the last twenty minutes.

But if you haven't started yet, this is important.

I'm a bit worried you might be having problems.

You know, because weather's not really your department.

So I just want to say that if there is a heap of extra inter-departmental paperwork involved, I'll help you with it.

I can do really neat writing if I have to.

If Matthew Conn's not flicking dust balls at me.

So if you're bogged down with forms and

reports, get some of them to me somehow, OK?

Also, you might be having doubts about whether it's OK to change the weather pattern of an entire district just cause one kid asks you to.

Don't worry.

Everyone round here wants the drought to end.

They're desperate for it.

I'll give you an example.

When Sergeant Crean chucked me out of the pool just now I tried to explain why he had to let me back in.

'My guardian angel supplied the water,' I said, 'but he's busy now on an even bigger project so I've got to help him out and keep an eye on people and make sure they don't drown.'

Sergeant Crean wasn't convinced.

'Cathy Saxby's right,' he said. 'You are mental.'

He went back in.

I was about to follow him and tell him about my training programme and how once I've won lots of gold diving trophies it'll be his responsibility to guard them at our place and he'll probably get promoted to inspector.

Then something hit me on the back of the head.

I felt it splatter against the top of my neck

and when I looked down there were red bits on my shoulders.

It was a tomato.

I turned round.

Carla was standing there scowling at me.

'That's for Enid,' she said.

Or something like that.

It was a bit hard to understand because she had a can opener in her mouth.

Before I could ask her to speak more clearly she chucked another one.

'And this is for Roald.'

That's what it sounded like.

The tomato hit me in the chest.

Bits of it splashed up under my chin and the rest slid down my front.

I was numb with shock.

'Hang on,' I said. 'I don't even know these people.'

Carla glared at me through her curls and suddenly I realised why her eyes were glinting so much.

They had tears in them.

She took another tomato from the can she was holding and got ready to chuck it.

My T-shirt was sodden and I could feel tomato juice soaking into my swimmers. I hate canned tomatoes. That's the trouble with living in a drought-affected area, fresh vegies are so expensive.

116

I had to get the can away from Carla.

Before I could move, Carla's mum pulled up in their ute.

'Carla,' said Mrs Fiami sharply, 'get in the car and stop wasting food.'

Then she saw me.

Her eyes narrowed.

'Sorry,' she said to Carla, 'I thought you were wasting it. I didn't realise you were putting it to good use.'

Carla threw the whole can of tomatoes at me.

I ducked and they splattered against the side of the pool kiosk.

'That's for Paul, Judy, Gillian, R.L., Emily, A.A., Lewis, Anna and Louisa May,' shouted Carla tearfully.

I think those were the names.

I stared at her, desperately trying to think of a big family that had been chucked off their land lately.

'They're all gunna die,' yelled Carla, 'thanks to your dad.'

Mrs Fiami revved the ute and as they drove off I caught a glimpse of a big box of ammo in the back.

For a gut-churning sec I thought that Carla had persuaded a whole lot of her rellies to help the Malleys shoot Dad, then turn their guns on themselves.

Dopey, I know, but the shock I was feeling

must have been stopping the blood getting to my brain.

Then the blood must have started flowing again because I suddenly remembered something I'd heard about Carla.

How she gives names to all the sheep at her place.

Then I understood.

My guts stopped churning and just lay there, still and sad.

There's something farmers have to do in droughts, Doug, when they can't afford feed for their animals. It saves the animals suffering hunger and starvation.

No wonder Carla was so upset.

The Fiamis are going to shoot their sheep.

'Stop,' I yelled, running after the ute, 'you don't have to, the drought's gunna be over soon.'

They were too far away to hear.

That's why I'm hurrying out to their place.

To try and let them know.

I just wish their place wasn't so far away on foot.

Anyway, Doug, you can see how relieved they'll be when you end the drought.

If I can get there in time.

And even if I can't there are heaps of other families like them.

So if you're having doubts, don't.

Chapter Twenty-two

As soon as I got to the Fiamis' fence, I saw them.

Sheep.

Skinny and dusty and not in a very good mood, but alive.

Yes, I thought, I'm in time.

And even though my feet hurt and my face was burning and I had dried tomato sludge on my neck, I jumped over the fence with a whoop of joy.

The sheep took a few steps back.

'G'day,' I said to the sheep.

They took a few more steps back.

Then a thought hit me.

What if these were only some of the sheep?

Sent over here so they wouldn't be mentally scarred by the awful violence taking place on the other side of the property.

'Is there an Enid here?' I asked.

The sheep looked at me blankly.

'How about Roald?'

No one put up their hoof.

'Paul?' I said, 'R.L.? Lousia May?'

The sheep nearest me did a poo and for a sec I thought she'd recognised the name, but she hadn't.

I listened carefully for distant gunfire, but all I could hear was my heart pounding.

I hurried over to the house.

Luckily it was quite close to the fence, only about two kilometres, so I was there in about fifteen minutes.

There didn't seem to be anybody around.

I still couldn't hear any gunfire, so I crept round to the back of the house hoping I wouldn't run into anything bad.

Like dead sheep.

Or Mrs Fiami pointing a gun at me.

Or Carla with a giant can of tomatoes.

I didn't run into any of those.

What I ran into made me stare and blink to make sure my eyes were working properly.

It was a boat.

The first boat I'd ever seen in real life apart from on telly.

I went over to it.

It was pretty big, longer than Dad's four-wheel drive probably, with yellow and blue paint that was peeling off and a cabin with a window and a windscreen wiper.

And it was propped up on bricks.

'Don't touch that!' yelled a voice.

Carla came out of the house scowling.

I was relieved to see she didn't have any vegetables with her.

'That's my Dad's,' she said. 'Get away from it.'

I got away from it and remembered why I was there.

'Have you done it yet?' I asked anxiously.

My mouth was drier than a garden hose.

'Done what?' said Carla.

'Shot the sheep,' I said.

Carla didn't blink behind her curls.

'We're waiting a couple of days,' she said. 'Mum's gunna plead with the bank one more time to lend us more money for sheep feed.'

'You don't have to,' I said. 'The drought'll be over any day. Doug's fixing it.'

Carla stared at me, still not blinking.

She seemed to be in shock.

I tried to help her snap out of it.

'So,' I said, 'want to come swimming?'

'I hate swimming,' she said.

I tried to think what to say next.

'Prefer sailing, eh?' I said weakly.

'I hate sailing,' she said.

We looked at each other.

'Plus,' she said, 'I hate bull.'

For a sec I didn't know what she meant.

'Angel bull,' she said with a scowl.

Don't take it personally, Doug, she was upset.

'Did you think angels were bull when you had one?' I asked her.

She had a think.

Her eyes went darker and glintier and I knew they were filling with tears.

'Not at first,' she said. 'Not till he dumped me.'

'Are you absolutely sure he dumped you?' I said. 'He might have just lost your address.'

Carla looked at me like I was something she'd found growing in her lunch box.

OK, it was a dopey idea.

I had a better one.

'Doug could get his secretary to make inquiries and find out what happened to him,' I said. 'What was his name?'

'Dad,' said Carla quietly.

I stared at her.

'And I know what happened to him,' she said. 'He fell off his fishing boat and drowned.'

She picked up a rock and hurled it at the boat.

'So don't waste my time with bull,' she said, picking up another rock and facing me. 'If you're gunna be a pin brain, rack off.'

I tried to think of something to say, something to make her feel better, but before I could Mrs Fiami stuck her head out of the house and glared at me.

I racked off.

122

I wasn't gunna bother you with this, Doug, you being so busy, but I've been thinking about it most of the way home and there's something I think you should know.

Remember I told you once about a dopey thought I'd had?

About Dad rescuing me?

Forget I ever thought it.

Poor old Carla thought her dad could be a guardian angel and look what happened.

I'm lucky, I've got the real thing.

I'll stick with you, Doug.

Chapter Twenty-three

Sorry to interrupt again, Doug, but I just want to let you know things are looking pretty grim for Carla's sheep.

I decided to have a word to Dad about them.

It was almost dark when I got home and I thought Mum and Dad would chuck a fit.

Luckily they were doing paperwork so they weren't completely on the ball.

'Have a good splash, love?' said Mum, barely looking up. 'Get your new swimmers wet?'

I nodded and felt them sticking to my buttocks and hoped we weren't having tinned tomatoes for tea.

'Any clues yet,' said Dad, 'about who's behind the water?'

I opened my mouth to tell him, then closed it again.

One thing at a time, as we're always telling Gran.

'I reckon it was Martians,' said Gran without looking up from the telly.

'Kind-hearted lotto winner more like,' said Mum, 'touched by the way a group of misguided but determined young people had a punt.'

While Gran had a coughing fit and I banged her on the back, I explained to Dad about Carla's sheep and how if the bank lent Carla's mum more money they'd probably win an animal welfare award, plus get some good chops later on.

Dad gave a big sigh and rubbed his hand wearily over his face and knocked his paperclips over.

'I'm sorry, Mitch,' he said. 'I wish I could help, but the bank won't be lending Mrs Fiami any more money. She owes them a stack already.'

I pleaded with him.

Dad said he'd swing it if he could, but he knew he couldn't.

I saw the way his shoulders were slumped and I knew he couldn't as well.

'Hopeless,' muttered Gran.

'Don't worry,' I said, 'I'll ask Doug.'

Dad went out of the room.

Mum winced and rubbed her tummy.

I felt terrible I'd even mentioned it.

I should have known it'd be a waste of time.

I should have come straight to you, Doug.

Which is what I'm doing now.

Don't get me wrong, I'm not asking you to rush things.

As Gran always says, if you rush things you won't do a good job and you'll probably give yourself a stressed ligament.

On the other hand there are some sheep around here who are pretty desperate for a feed and a wash and who'll be getting a bullet instead if it doesn't rain very soon.

I can't sleep.

My body's tired, specially my feet and neck, but my brain won't knock off.

When I first went to bed I kept thinking I could hear rain, but the noises just turned out to be the fridge, then Gran making popcorn, then the wind blowing dust against the house, then Gran frying an egg.

Mum got up and made Gran go to bed, then came in to see if I was being kept awake by the wind noise.

Dust storms make people pretty nervous in these parts. As well as over-exciting livestock they make car engines go out of tune and play havoc with false teeth.

I told Mum not to worry, that you were keeping an eye on us, Doug.

I know that's not strictly true at the moment, but I don't want her to worry.

Mum gave a big sigh, of relief I suppose.

'Go to sleep, Mitch,' she said softly.

I wished she'd said it to my brain.

Immediately she'd gone it started thinking about Carla.

And her Dad.

And his boat.

And the bricks propping it up.

At first I reckoned it was just desperate for subjects to think about.

Then I remembered something that woke my guts up, and my lungs, and that bit of your chest that thumps when your heart beats fast.

The colour of the bricks.

Dirty pink with black bits.

Exactly the same colour, I suddenly remembered, as the brick that was hurled through our window.

And the same shape.

And the same size.

I tried to stop my brain thinking the next thought.

It wouldn't.

I had a vision of Carla chucking the brick.

I should feel angry, but I just feel like crying.

You'd feel like crying too, Doug, if you only had one friend and it turned out she'd chucked a brick at you and your family.

I've just taken a deep breath and told my

chest to go back to sleep and my brain to stop being so suspicious.

Heaps of people in the district have got dirty pink bricks with black bits.

The bush fire brigade hut's completely built of them.

So's Mr Howard the brigade captain's barbeque.

OK, they're all cemented down, but still.

Anyway, it could have been Carla's mum.

I'm making my brain think about something else now to cheer me up. How great it'll be when the drought's broken and Dad doesn't have to dob people any more and we can all become respected and well-liked members of the community.

I'm thinking about my birthday party next year.

Heaps of kids watching me do championship dives into the pool we'll probably install in the back yard.

Dad next to the fountain and the waterfall juggling ping-pong balls with his mouth.

Gran juggling chocolate crackles with hers.

It's gunna be great, eh Doug?

Chapter Twenty-four

When I woke up and saw how late it was, I rushed out to the kitchen to gobble some Rice Bubbles so I could get down to the pool and do some dives before the water filled up with farmers.

Dad was at the kitchen table in purple undies.

I didn't know where to look.

I was glad Gran wasn't up.

She can be really cruel about Dad's underwear.

Don't be offended, Doug, if you wear purple undies.

I bet they look cool on you.

It's just that they look pretty tragic on over-weight Bank Liaison Officers.

I kept my eyes on the Rice Bubbles.

Then I remembered something.

Dad doesn't have any purple undies.

'Don't guts yourself,' said Dad, pointing to the big bowl I was filling. 'I'm not giving a diving lesson to a bloke who's gunna sink on me.'

I realised they were purple swimmers.

I stared at him in amazement, partly because I'd never seen him in swimmers before and partly because I couldn't believe what I'd just heard.

For a sec I thought being up on the diving board yesterday had damaged my eardrums.

It hadn't.

'I've been thinking about you fancying yourself as a diving champ,' said Dad. 'If a bloke from these parts wants to take on the world at that caper, I reckon he could use a few tips.'

I felt like doing cartwheels across the kitchen and hugging him.

Except there was something I had to ask first.

'Um ... Dad,' I said, 'do you know anything about diving?'

Dad grinned and hooked his thumbs into the waistband of his swimmers.

'I might be just a mild-mannered Bank Liaison Officer to you, digger,' he said, 'but I've been around and done a few things, OK?'

I reckon sometimes we have to trust people, eh Doug?

We're in the car on the way to the pool now, and I've just told Dad about you filling it.

He went quiet for a bit.

Then he changed the subject and explained why Rice Bubbles don't help you float, even if you eat them dry. It's got to do with digestive juices and compacting.

I'm glad he took the time to explain that.

I reckon if a person's good with the theory, there's a good chance he'll be OK with the practical stuff too.

The pool was just as crowded as yesterday.

All the Wicks's were there, climbing onto each other's shoulders and falling off with shrieks.

Not their dogs, but.

The whole pool was full of shouting, splashing people.

As me and Dad walked in, I wondered how Dad was gunna give me a diving lesson if there weren't any vacant patches of water.

I needn't have worried.

As soon as Dad stood at the edge of the pool and started showing me arm positions, the people in the water stopped splashing and shouting and started muttering to each other and backing away.

They're still doing it.

There's a patch of water in front of Dad big enough for an elephant to dive into.

Dad doesn't seem to have noticed.

He's probably concentrating on other things.

Like keeping his balance that close to the edge of the pool without falling in.

Oh, no.

He's fallen in.

Everyone's laughing.

People can be so predictable.

Just cause a person's been talking about the importance of keeping his arms and legs together and his neck and ankles straight, and then he's slipped and fallen into the water with his arms and legs and neck and ankles all over the place, people think it's funny.

Dad's very sensibly staying under water till the unkind laughter stops.

Jeez, he's got good lungs.

He's been under there for ages.

It's hard to see exactly where he is cause the water's pretty murky from the dust storm.

People are starting to look anxious.

I'm starting to feel anxious.

Dad's not that good at holding his breath, I've seen him try and do it after he's hit his thumb with a hammer.

Dad, where are you?

People are shouting and swimming towards where he disappeared into the water.

Doug, drop what you're doing, this is urgent.

Chapter Twenty-five

Thanks, Doug.

Thanks for moving so fast.

Another second and I'd have jumped into the water and then I might never have found Dad with so many people swimming around yelling.

Making him float to the surface was a great idea.

It meant I could be the one to grab the back of his swimmers and drag him out.

It's much less embarrassing to be rescued by your own son than by a bunch of people who hate your guts, even if they do have to help with a bit of pushing.

I reckon Dad handled it really well.

After he'd finished coughing up pool water, he thanked everyone and pretended he didn't hear them muttering things like 'stay out of the water you cretin'.

I was proud of him.

Right up till we got to the car.

'Well,' he said, rubbing the bruise on his forehead where he'd banged it on the concrete on his way into the pool, 'not such a bad start, eh?'

I didn't know what to say.

Dad grinned.

'Next time,' he said, 'I'll leave my shoes on for better grip.'

I tried to smile.

'Few more lessons,' said Dad, punching me in the shoulder, 'and you'll be diving like a champ.'

I was trying to think of a way to tell him that we'd both be better off without the lessons when he put his arm round my shoulders.

'You and me,' he said.

I think I knew what he was gunna say next because my insides suddenly felt like they were doing a reverse double somersault off a thousand-metre cliff.

'We don't need any dopey old wizards, gremlins or angels,' he said, 'do we mate?'

Sorry, Doug, that's what he said.

I could hardly breathe.

I waited for my mouth to stop having spasms of indignation so I could tell him how not only did you just save his life, you're pretty close to saving the lives of six hundred sheep.

He didn't give me time.

'Mitch,' he said, 'I want you to stop filling your head with nonsense about this Doug character.'

'Sorry Dad,' I said, 'I can't do that.'

His arm dropped away from my shoulders.

'I'm not asking you,' he said. 'I'm telling you.'

I didn't say anything.

I was wondering whether angels are allowed to adopt kids.

'Well?' he said.

His face was going as dark as his bruise.

I could see it was pointless trying to argue.

I just shook my head.

'Jeez,' exploded Dad. 'Why won't anyone listen to me?'

He grabbed my shoulders and squeezed them hard.

'I forbid you,' he shouted, his face very close to mine, 'to talk about Doug, think about Doug, play with Doug, draw pictures of Doug, write letters to Doug, dream about Doug, invite Doug to your birthday party or have diving lessons with Doug.'

Then he got in the car and drove off.

It's the pressure, Doug.

The pressure of being the most hated man in town.

It's getting to him.

It's only natural.

135

My legs have almost stopped shaking.

When they have I'm gunna go home and talk to him.

I reckon he'll calm down when I remind him that if it wasn't for you, people would probably have just stood around this arvo and watched him drown.

When I got home, Mum and Gran were in the kitchen.

Mum went gastric.

'You can be a very selfish boy, Mitch,' she yelled.

Gran stood up for me.

Except because she's old she did it sitting down.

'Don't blame him,' she muttered through a mouthful of muesli.

'I am blaming him,' yelled Mum, 'because he knows the pressure Noel's under and he still carries on with these ridiculous fairy stories.'

Gran had a small coughing fit.

I think it was mostly guilt.

'Where is Dad?' I asked after I'd banged Gran on the back.

'He's taken a Panadol and gone to bed,' said Mum.

'Hopeless,' muttered Gran.

Mum gave a big sigh and pushed me down into a chair next to Gran.

'Mr Grimmond from the bank is coming up from the city day after tomorrow,' she said. 'Dad reckons Mr Grimmond's coming to give him the sack.'

The kitchen spun a bit.

I could see why Mum had sat me down.

Even Gran looked shocked.

'Why?' I managed to ask.

Mum sighed again.

'Dad wrote a report on the Fiami property,' she said. 'Mrs Fiami owes the bank a heap of money and she's going broke and can't pay them. Dad knew the bank'd take her farm if they found out so he left it out of the report.'

'Good on him,' said Gran.

I thought so too, but I was puzzled.

'Why did he do that for the Fiamis,' I asked, 'when he's never done it for anyone else?'

'He's done it a bit for other families,' said Mum, 'but he went further for Carla and her mum because he didn't want you to lose the only friend you've got.'

I stood up to go and give Dad a hug.

I'd been feeling numb since he disappeared into the water this arvo, but suddenly I just wanted to throw my arms round him.

Then a thought hit me.

'With all this on his plate,' I said, 'why did he try and give me a diving lesson today?'

Mum sat down and closed her eyes, but I

137

could still see tears squeezing out from under her lids.

'Because,' she whispered, 'he's your dad.'

That's when my own eyes started to get hot and drippy.

Mum pulled me onto her lap and put her arms round me and we sat like that until Gran lit a cigarette and inhaled a piece of muesli.

OK, Doug.

I know this is the point where you'd normally leap into action.

But this time I don't want you to.

You've had enough interruptions and it's more important you finish the drought job.

I'll take care of this bank bloke.

After Mum had gone to look after Dad, I asked Gran for a hand.

'It'd be a tragedy if Dad got the boot now,' I said, 'before the drought breaks. He'd be remembered forever as a mean and nasty person.'

Gran agreed.

'What we need to do,' I said, 'is get hold of Mr Grimmond between the airstrip and the bank and keep him somewhere till it rains.'

Gran stared at me.

'The roof of the school hall,' I suggested.

Gran coughed and spluttered so hard that muesli pinged off the microwave.

'That's kidnapping,' she said.

'OK,' I said desperately, 'we could bribe him.'

'What with?' said Gran. 'Empty soft drink bottles?'

I had an idea.

'Your savings,' I said. 'Dad'll pay you back once the drought's broken and the bank can afford to give him a raise.'

'Sorry,' said Gran. 'I'm skint.'

I knew why.

'Dumb cigarettes,' I said. 'They shouldn't make 'em so expensive.'

Gran looked hurt and took a deep wheezy breath.

She started to say something.

'It's OK, Gran,' I said gently. 'You don't have to make excuses. We'll kidnap him.'

Gran put her spoon down.

'In my experience,' she said, 'there's something that works better than bribery or kidnapping.'

I hoped she wasn't gunna say murder.

'Friendship,' she said.

I thought about it.

I thought about Carla and how good that was while it lasted.

I reckon Gran's right.

This is just to let you know, Doug, that everything's under control.

I won't be going to sleep tonight till I've

figured out how I can get to be such good mates with Mr Grimmond that he'll keep Dad in the job and give him extra money to lend Mrs Fiami to keep her going till you've ended the drought.

Chapter Twenty-six

Just a quick update, Doug.

I was awake most of last night, but I couldn't crack it.

The idea didn't come to me till this morning at school.

Even then I was so tired I almost missed it.

Ms Dorrit made the announcement in assembly and it just rolled over me like mineral water off a duck's back.

Then all the other kids started cheering and yakking to each other excitedly.

'Swimming carnival!' they were saying. 'We're having a swimming carnival!'

Suddenly I was listening so hard I could hear the sheets of paper rustling in Ms Dorrit's manila folder.

'. . . very fortunate,' she was saying. 'The council were going to close the pool from today on account of the filter being clogged by Saturday night's dust storm. However they've agreed to leave it open one more day so tomorrow we can have our first school swimming carnival for eight years.'

Everyone cheered again, including me.

'So,' said Ms Dorrit sternly, 'make the most of it.'

That's exactly what I'm doing, Doug.

I worked on the idea all day at school, and as soon as I got home I put it to Dad.

'Invite Mr Grimmond to the swimming carnival,' I said. 'Then, after I've won the diving and he's mega impressed and wants to be my friend, we can tell him about my future diving career and how I'm available for sponsorship.'

As Dad put his cup of tea down he knocked the spoon out of the sugar bowl so I could tell he was interested.

'If the bank's sponsoring me and I'm gunna be getting them top publicity all over the world,' I said, 'they're not gunna sack you, are they? Plus if I offer to put their logo on my swimmers I reckon they'll be nicer to the folks round here.'

'Brilliant,' said Gran.

Dad didn't say anything.

Mum put her hand gently on my arm.

'What if you don't win the diving, love?' she said.

I didn't want to mention your name, Doug, and get Dad ropeable again.

142

So I just tried to look very confident.

'I can do it,' I said. 'I know I can.'

'He'll have a punt,' said Gran. 'You can't ask more than that.'

Mum didn't look convinced.

Dad didn't say anything.

My insides sagged.

Then Mum put her hand on Dad's arm.

'Wouldn't hurt, Noel, would it?' she said. 'If Mr Grimmond sees what a top little community we've got here, he might be easier on all of us.'

Dad thought about it.

'Worth a punt,' he said.

Gran nearly choked on her tea.

I've just done a few practice dives off the wardrobe and I haven't lost the knack, Doug.

So I won't need to bother you again till I'm up on the diving board tomorrow.

Chapter Twenty-seven

This is gunna be the best day of my whole life,
I just know it, Doug.

It is so far, and I've only been awake four
seconds.

When I opened my eyes, the first thing I
spotted was Grandad's medal on my pillow.

I stared at the gleaming metal diver soaring
over the writing and my insides soared too.

Then I glanced out the window.

I don't reckon I'd have known for sure
what I was seeing if Dad hadn't been yelling
in the front yard.

'Clouds! Clouds!'

I'm dragging on my swimmers and rushing
outside.

Jeez, there's lots of them.

Ten, fifteen, twenty at least.

They're huge.

One of them's covering the sun.

There's one that looks like Gran blowing
smoke out of her ear.

Doug, you're a genius.

Everyone's out in the street in their pyjamas, pointing and shouting.

And arguing.

Daryl the postie's telling Gran clouds don't mean anything, there were clouds here six years ago and they were dry as a wombat's wellies.

Gran's telling him not to be such a misery.

I reckon she knows, Doug.

Even though she has spells when she loses her grip, I reckon she knows you're on the job and you're gunna crack it.

She's offering to lend Daryl her umbrella.

Daryl's getting so worked up he's not even paying attention to his job.

He's just lobbed a letter into our postbox and missed and now it's blowing across the front yard.

I'd better grab it.

I hope this isn't gunna be the worst day of my whole life.

It was going great until a minute ago.

Everyone in town's come to the swimming carnival.

I know that's probably so they could get out of work and stare up at the clouds, but at least they're here.

Most important of all, Mr Grimmond's here with Mum and Dad and Gran.

That's him down there in the suit and tie telling Gran he doesn't want a chocolate crackle.

Nobody's staring up at the clouds now, but.

They're staring up at me.

And pointing and yelling and carrying on.

They've been doing it ever since Ms Dorrit announced the diving would be first and I jumped up and sprinted for the diving board.

I didn't wait for her to explain that the diving would have to be off the side because the water's too shallow to use the high board.

I jumped on the ladder and started climbing up before anyone could stop me.

I was gunna wait till I reached the board before I gave you a hoi to watch out for me, Doug. You know, so I could dive without hitting the bottom and having my brains leak out into the pool.

I'm not there yet but I've just realised something.

It's such a dopey thing to have done, I'm almost ashamed to admit it.

I've got Gran's letter in my swimmers.

When I picked it up in the front yard earlier Gran was busy yelling at Daryl the postie. She gets really irate if she's interrupted when she's arguing, so I stuck the letter down my swimmers for safe keeping.

And forgot it.

Until now.

I don't know what to do.

The envelope's got a window in it so I can tell it's important.

If I dive it'll get sodden.

If I leave it on the board it'll blow away.

Mr Tristos and the other teachers are climbing the ladder.

I'm on the board now, but I can't think straight with the noise of the kids down there cheering and the parents yelling.

I'm opening the letter. I'm reading it so at least I can tell Gran what was in it.

Except it isn't a letter, it's a receipt.

From a transport company.

To Gran.

Thanking her for the money.

The money for the three tankers of water.

Oh, Jeez.

Doug, I need to know something really quickly now because Mr Tristos is nearly halfway up the ladder.

Did you make Gran send the water?

Or did she do it all by herself?

I'm confused, Doug, and I don't want to be.

I've got a crook feeling in my guts and it's not just cause I scraped my tummy on a step climbing up.

I need to know it was you who sent the water, Doug.

I need to know you're still looking after me.

It's urgent.

I'm on a very high diving board.

I've never done a high dive before into real water.

The water's a long way down and there isn't enough of it.

Mum and Dad are sitting down there with Mr Grimmond and everyone's depending on me.

I've got to dive.

Tell me you're still looking after me, Doug.

Mr Tristos has only got six steps left to climb.

Give me a sign, Doug.

Anything'll do.

A bird winking at me.

A cloud in the shape of a thumbs up.

Only three steps left.

I've got to dive now.

That black cloud over on the horizon looks a bit like a thumbs up.

Either that or a tombstone.

I guess I'll know in about five secs.

See ya, Doug.

Arms ... legs ... focus ...

Mr Tristos is so close I can feel drops of his sweat splashing on me.

Wait a sec.

148

Those drops.
They aren't from Mr Tristos.
They're from the sky.

RRRRRRRRRRRRRRRRRRRRRRRR
AAAAAAAAAAAAAAAAAAAAAAAAA
IIIIIIIIIIIIIIIIIIIIIIIIIIIIIIIIIIIIIIIIIIIIIIIII
NNNNNNNNNNNNNNNNNNNNNNNN
!!

Chapter Twenty-eight

I would have dived, Doug.

I wanted to.

OK, at first I just wanted to stand there with my head back and feel the rain splashing on my face while my legs stopped wobbling.

But I got the urge to dive again after a few secs.

Once Mr Tristos started hugging me and dancing round on the board and singing.

Trouble was, I couldn't get back to the edge because the more Mr Tristos's clothes got sodden with rain, the heavier he was to drag.

And when Mrs Chaplin finally made it to the top and he let go and started dancing with her, so many ecstatic people down below had jumped into the pool there wasn't a clear patch of water.

I'm not complaining, Doug.

Now it's raining there'll be heaps of water to dive into.

Thanks to you.

And this time I'm gunna make it up to you, Doug.

For doubting you.

I'm gunna make sure everyone knows you're the hero who broke the drought.

I've told as many people as I can, Doug.

I'm not sure it sank in with everyone.

Sometimes it's hard to get people's attention when they're doing cartwheels in puddles and dancing on car roofs and kissing pot plants, but I did my best.

I got some people's attention, but.

They didn't actually say anything when I told them about your angel powers, but I could see they were impressed.

And grateful, Doug.

Like me.

I'd forgotten how noisy rain is.

Which is another reason why I'm having trouble getting some people's attention.

For example, in the car going out to the airstrip I told Dad, Mum, Gran and Mr Grimmond from the bank that you'd made it rain, Doug.

Nobody said a thing.

The noise of the rain must have drowned out my words.

Funny but, when we got to the airstrip and

Dad told Mr Grimmond that the farmers would soon be able to pay their debts and Mr Grimmond told Dad to keep up the good work and Dad told Mr Grimmond to hurry up or his plane might not be able to take off, the rain didn't drown out their words.

Oh well.

Perhaps I've strained my voice with too much yelling for joy.

I gave Gran her receipt when we got home.

It was pretty soggy, but she knew what it was.

I didn't say anything about you making her spend her life savings, Doug, in case she got irate and choked on her toast.

I just told her she's the best Gran in the whole world and gave her a hug.

She didn't say anything at first, just hugged me back.

Then she said, 'We're quits now, eh?'

I smiled and nodded even though I didn't understand what she meant.

She must have seen I didn't.

'I got you started on Doug,' she said, 'so I reckoned it was up to me to finish it. I reckoned the best way to convince you Doug isn't real was to fill the pool myself and prove you don't need him.'

I stared at her.

'I thought I couldn't survive without Grandad once,' she said, 'but I can.'

'Gran,' I said quietly, 'Doug is real. He made it rain.'

She started going on about low pressure fronts and high pressure fronts colliding in the upper atmosphere.

Poor old Gran.

People that kind-hearted shouldn't have to suffer the indignity of losing their grip and going unintelligible.

Mum and Dad and Gran have been explaining that it takes twenty-four hours of heavy rain for water to start soaking in to drought-struck land.

They reckon it'd be well and truly doing that now, Doug.

'I reckon those paddocks'll be almost as waterlogged as you soon,' Gran's just said.

I'm in the bath.

I don't mind her being here, but.

I've got the water so deep she can't see anything.

Two days of non-stop rain.

You're a genius, Doug.

Dad reckons the farmers' dams are filling and there are green shoots coming up at the Wilkinsons' place.

That's what he overheard at the Gas 'N' Gobble.

The farmers aren't actually speaking to him yet, but they will be soon now he's off their backs.

And once the rain stops and we have the swimming carnival and my diving career takes off, he'll be a hero.

Three days.

Doug, this is wonderful.

I had no idea you'd do it this well.

The river's flowing really fast now.

I'd forgotten this town even had a river.

We had a class excursion down there today and I tried to get everyone to sign a petition.

When I've got a hundred signatures I'll present it to the council.

It's to get the name changed from the Strathpine River to the Doug River.

Not many of the kids wanted to sign it today, but that was probably because the rain was making the letters go runny.

Four days.

Boy, Doug, when you break a drought you really break a drought.

PE was cancelled today because the school hall roof's leaking.

On the way home I went to the video store for Gran, and guess what?

Mr Bullock's cleared out his Water section.

Now it's called Sun and Sand.

Troy and Brent Malley were there picking up *Desert Killers* for their folks.

When I asked them to sign the petition they got really nervous and stood very close to Mr Bullock.

Troy said he'd give me half a Mars Bar if I'd leave them alone.

Pretty weird, eh?

Mum reckons rain can affect people like that.

Five days of rain.

Unbelievable.

Actually Doug, five days will probably be enough.

We probably won't need much more rain after today.

You know, given that all the dams are full.

And all the water tanks have been overflowing for three days.

And there are seven trucks bogged on the highway outside town.

And Gran's muesli has started sprouting.

Don't get me wrong, Doug, we're very grateful.

But today's probably the last day we'll need rain as such.

~

Doug, I know you like to do a job really well.

That's why you're the world's number one angel.

Well you've done this job really, really well.

Six days non-stop rain is a top effort.

But it's definitely enough.

OK?

Thanks.

Emergency call to Doug.

The main street's under water.

So's the front yard.

It's started coming into the house.

Stop the rain, Doug.

Please.

This is an urgent message to Doug's secretary.

If he's off saving a school camp from a killer spider or something, could you let him know that the rain he started on the Mitch Webber job eight days ago has got totally out of hand.

Gran's bed is soaked.

I've had to put everything in my room on top of the wardrobe.

Mum's had to put all the money at the bank into plastic bags.

The town's being evacuated.

Get him back here.

Now.

~

I don't understand, Doug.

Where are you?

Can't you see what's happening?

Or is the rain getting in your eyes too?

The whole town's queueing up to get into army helicopters.

Everyone's wet and muddy and miserable.

Most of the grown-ups have been up for the last two nights filling sandbags to try and stop the river bursting its banks.

They've had to give up.

There's a heap of water on its way down from up north and there's just not enough sandbags in town.

Even if we used bags of sheep pellets and disposable nappies we couldn't stop it.

So we're all standing here on the sports oval up to our knees in water.

Nobody's saying anything, but I can tell what everyone's thinking.

The same as me.

Why have you abandoned us, Doug?

Chapter Twenty-nine

Looks like me and Dad are history.

Dunno why I'm even telling you this, Doug.

Habit, I guess.

At least it gives my brain something to do instead of panic.

Brains don't panic as much when they're up to their necks in work.

That's what Gran reckons.

I'm gunna listen to her more from now on.

I reckon I should have listened to her more when she was trying to tell me about you.

Anyway, I've listened to her about brains, which is why I gave mine a job to do while we were waiting for the helicopters to arrive.

I made it try to cheer me up and make me forget about the rain running down the back of my neck by thinking that at least Carla wasn't in my queue saying 'I told you.'

Then I looked at the other queues.

She wasn't in any of those either.

'Dad,' I said, 'Carla and her mum aren't here.'

Dad looked at me with a grim wet face.

'Neither are the Wilkinsons or the Malleys,' he said, 'but we can't worry about them, Mitch, we've got our own problems.'

I looked at him and Mum and Gran.

The only problems I could see were that Dad's green garbage bag raincoat was a hopeless fit and Mum was sad about leaving her computer and dartboard behind and Gran was grumpy because she'd spent all her savings on water and now we were up to our knees in it.

'Should have spent it on beer,' she was muttering.

I told Dad about Carla's mum's ute and how it never started properly if condensation got into the carby.

'That's just a few drops of water,' I said. 'Imagine what a flood'll do.'

'Mitch,' said Dad, 'forget it.'

I couldn't.

'Carla's mum wanted to buy a new ute,' I said, 'but the bank wouldn't lend her the money.'

Dad looked like he wished he was somewhere else.

Africa or somewhere.

Then he had a muttered conversation with Mum.

Mum nodded.

159

Gran slapped him on the back.

I was so dazed at seeing this that I was slow off the mark when Dad started sloshing his way across the oval.

'Wait,' I yelled, splashing after him. 'I'm coming too.'

He started to send me back, then something made him change his mind.

Perhaps he thought if I came, Doug, you'd be coming too.

Big joke.

We went over to where Dad had tied the four-wheel drive to the war memorial with the winch cable to stop it being swept away.

Dad untied it and we headed out of town towards Carla's place.

The road was hard to see under the water but Dad knows the district like the back of his clipboard so we were right.

For a while.

Then I noticed something.

The water wasn't just splashing up onto the bullbar any more, sometimes it was foaming over the bullbar onto the bonnet.

'Slow down,' I said to Dad.

'We're only doing twenty k's,' said Dad. 'It's not us.'

I knew what he meant.

The water was getting deeper.

Normally at that stage I'd have asked you to

160

keep an eye on us Doug, but there didn't seem much point.

Instead I tried to keep Dad's spirits up.

'These four-wheel drives are great, aren't they?' I said. 'The way they keep going through anything.'

Dad grunted.

The engine coughed.

The four-wheel drive stopped.

Dad's been out there fiddling under the bonnet and swearing for ages now.

I've been up on the roof for a squiz around but all I could see was water.

The rain's stopped but the water's still rising.

Another third of a gearstick and it'll be over the car seat.

I blame myself.

I should never have got Dad to try and do a rescue.

Oh well, Doug.

Or Doug's secretary.

Or Doug's answering machine.

Or whoever's listening.

If anyone is.

Which I doubt.

At least Carla's not here to say 'I told you.'

'I told you.'

As soon as I heard Carla's voice I spun round.

161

And banged my head on the roof of the car.

I'd forgotten I was sitting on the back of the seat.

My eyes went funny for a bit and I could have sworn there was a boat coming towards us.

A blue and yellow boat.

With a huge outboard motor.

And a highly trained State Emergency Service rescue team.

Then my eyes cleared and I saw what it really was.

A blue and yellow boat.

With two oars flapping.

And two people arguing.

'I told you we were going the right way,' Carla was shouting. 'There's Mitch's dad's four-wheel drive. We must be close to town.'

'So where are the houses?' yelled Carla's mum. 'Where's the Gas 'N' Gobble?'

After me and Dad finished telling them how pleased we were to see them and we climbed into the boat, and Mrs Fiami finished scowling and moved some kitchen utensils to make room, and Dad knocked one of the oars into the water and I grabbed it, and Dad sat down and knocked the other oar into the water and Carla grabbed it, Mrs Fiami sighed.

'My late husband was a fisherman,' she said. 'He'd have got us to town easy peasy.'

Dad stood up and knocked a frying pan into the water.

'Sorry,' he said.

I grabbed at it, but it sank.

Dad peered at the row of fence posts sticking out of the water.

'We go that way,' he said.

Mrs Fiami showed us how the oars worked. She and Carla took one.

Me and Dad took the other.

We started rowing.

Dad soon got the hang of it and we stopped going round in circles and headed off in the direction he told us.

Why am I telling you this, Doug?

When you're not even listening?

Just to let you know that we can look after ourselves, thank you very much.

The Wilkinsons were amazed to see us, partly because they're both over seventy and they don't get many visitors, and partly because of the boat.

'Amazing,' said Mr Wilkinson as we helped him off his roof. 'Don't see many of these little beauties this far from the sea.'

'I hate it,' said Mrs Fiami.

'Are you keen on fishing?' asked Mrs Wilkinson as Dad lifted her into the boat.

'I hate it,' said Mrs Fiami.

She explained she'd only kept the boat as evidence. Something to do with Mr Fiami's life insurance and a mongrel insurance company.

While Dad explained to the Wilkinsons that there wasn't room for all their carpets and chickens, I had a word to Carla.

She'd hardly made a sound since we got in the boat and I could see she was upset about something.

'Is it Roald and Enid,' I asked quietly, 'and the others?'

Sheep hate water even more than mayors do.

Carla shook her head.

'They're on our roof with the last of the feed,' she mumbled. 'They'll be right.'

She bit her lip.

'We left the photo album behind,' said Mrs Fiami sadly.

Carla's eyes glinted.

'With the only photos of her dad,' continued Mrs Fiami. She gave a sigh. 'It's probably history by now.'

Carla looked away.

I didn't know what to say.

Dad stood up and knocked a hall rug into the water.

'Sorry,' he said.

He peered at the fence posts.

'The Malleys' place is this way,' he said.

I thought of you, Doug, and how quickly you'd get us out of this.

Then I grabbed an oar and tried to think of a way to tell Carla that I know how she feels about being dumped.

The Malleys were amazed to see us too.

They stood on their roof and aimed rifles at us.

'Don't you bank buggers ever give up?' snarled Mr Malley.

Dad explained it wasn't an eviction, it was a rescue.

Mr Malley didn't look impressed.

Mrs Malley told Troy and Brent to stop snivelling.

Troy and Brent both went bright pink because they'd been hoping me and Carla wouldn't notice.

When they all got into the boat I could still see tears on Troy and Brent's cheeks.

While Dad explained to Mr and Mrs Malley that there wasn't room for all their guns, I gave Troy and Brent a sympathetic look.

'We'd have been OK,' mumbled Troy, 'if Dad hadn't accidentally shot the fuel line in the ute.'

Mrs Malley cuffed him round the head.

Dad stood up and knocked a double-barrelled shotgun into the water.

Mr Malley howled.
Dad didn't say anything.
He just squinted at the fence posts.
We're on our way to town now.

Chapter Thirty

The boat started leaking about halfway there.

Not a lot at first, but then more.

'It's the planks,' said Mrs Fiami. 'Some of them are a bit rotten.'

Everyone grabbed kitchen utensils and started scooping the water out.

Except me.

I'd had a thought.

A top fisherman like Mr Fiami must have kept stuff in his boat to repair leaks.

Plastic sealant and stuff.

I had a hunt around under people's feet.

Then Dad gave a yell.

The metal thing that kept his oar in place had popped out of the wood.

Mr Wilkinson grabbed it before it could fall in the water.

'There's a brick somewhere to knock it back in,' said Mrs Fiami. 'In the cabin, Mitch.'

I crawled into the little cabin and found the brick.

It was dirty pink with black bits.

I passed it down to Dad and hoped he wouldn't notice.

Then I realised Carla had been crouching next to me the whole time.

She took a deep breath and cleared her throat.

'When the bank wouldn't lend us money to buy feed,' she said quietly, 'I got very ropeable.'

She glanced nervously at me, and then at Dad, who was banging the metal thing in with the brick.

Dad looked like a man who was worrying about saving ten people from drowning, not worrying about broken windows from the past.

'Sorry,' said Carla softly.

I squeezed her arm to let her know I'd have done the same thing if my dad had drowned and my sheep were starving.

Then I saw something.

Behind Carla's head.

A sort of hole in the cabin wall.

It wasn't a rotten hole, it was a cut hole.

The sort of hole a person would make if they were looking for somewhere to store tubes of plastic sealant and their boat didn't have any drawers.

I stuck my hand in there, hoping it wasn't where Mr Fiami had stored the fish guts.

It wasn't.

Inside I felt something hard and square.

After a bit of juggling I lifted out a metal box that looked exactly like a tool box.

It was locked with a padlock.

Jeez, I thought, this must be really expensive plastic sealant.

Carla tapped me on the shoulder and handed me the brick.

For a sec I thought she was offering it to me to keep and chuck through her window when the flood was over.

Then I twigged.

I started whacking the padlock with it.

After a few whacks, the padlock broke and the lid flipped open.

Inside the box were some small metal hooks and a plastic bag and some sort of pistol.

Carla opened the bag.

I examined the pistol but it wasn't a sealant gun.

The plastic bag didn't have sealant in it either, just an old notebook.

'Mitch, Carla,' yelled Dad. 'Bail out some of this water or we won't make it.'

We've been scooping water for hours.

That's why I'm telling you all this, Doug or the man in the moon or whoever's listening, to take my mind off the pain in my arms.

And to block out Troy and Brent's sobbing.

And to let you know we are gunna make it.

Chapter Thirty-one

I just want to say, Doug or the man in the moon or whoever, that we would have made it.

If it hadn't been for the tidal wave.

When we reached town it was almost dark, but we could still see the roofs in the main street.

I felt like cheering, even though I had blisters from rowing and arm cramps from scooping.

Then Mrs Malley screamed.

For a sec I thought she'd seen a relative or a helicopter with dry towels on board.

Then Mr Malley screamed.

So did Troy, Brent and the Wilkinsons.

I spun round.

Moving towards us from the direction of the river, faster than ten cattle trucks having a drag, was a wall of water.

Roofs were disappearing under it.

'Hang on!' yelled Dad, and then it hit us.

Suddenly we were powering down the main street so fast that if Sergeant Crean had been on board we'd have been booked for sure.

And then just as suddenly it had gone, and we were left spinning round and round, all still screaming.

I opened my eyes.

The main street had gone too.

The only bit of town I could see was the diving board tower.

Water was pouring into the boat.

'Row,' yelled Dad. 'Head for the diving board.'

We all rowed frantically using oars, saucepans, rifles and hands.

Somehow we got there.

Dad made us all clamber onto the steps before he'd leave the boat.

For a sec I thought he'd left it too late.

'Dad!' I screamed as the boat sank.

Dad jumped for the steps.

He clanged onto them.

Once the steps had stopped shaking, and we had too, we climbed slowly up to the top.

Diving boards aren't made for ten people, so it's pretty crowded up here.

We're just sort of huddled together in the dark, listening for helicopters.

We haven't heard any yet, but they could

have been drowned out by Troy and Brent's
sobbing and Mrs Wilkinson's asthma.

And the noise of the water swirling past.

The diving board gives a shudder every now
and then.

I haven't said anything, but I keep thinking
about how crumbly the concrete is at the base
of the steps.

I think Dad might be thinking about that
too, because he muttered something a while
back.

He had his arms round me, and he must
have forgotten his mouth was so close to my
ears.

'OK Doug,' he said, 'I give in. Get us out
of this and I'll believe in you.'

I've been holding my breath for ages.

But you're not getting us out of it, are you,
Doug?

We're on our own, aren't we?

Well stuff you, Doug.

You had your chance and you blew it.

Now I'm gunna save us.

I just wish I didn't have to dive into that
dark swirling water.

If I can hold my breath long enough to get
down to the kiosk and back, I'll be right.

If.

Best not to think about it, as Gran says
when she's eating tripe.

Stand up quickly before Dad realises what's going on.

Arms.

Legs.

Quick focus.

And dive.

Oh no, my head's too far back.

My tummy's sticking too far out.

I'm doing a belly fl—

Chapter Thirty-two

I must have blacked out.

The belly flop must have winded me.

I don't get it.

I'm in the water, but I'm not sinking.

I can feel the current dragging at my feet, but I'm not moving.

What's this round my chest?

Arms.

Strong arms.

I can hardly breathe.

Doug?

You at last?

Is that you whispering in my ear?

Telling me I'm a stupid maniac?

No.

It's Dad.

He wants to know if I'm ok.

I can't speak.

Partly because Dad's squeezing so hard.

Partly because I'm crying.

Funny thing with us humans, Doug.
Mostly we cry when we're sad.
But sometimes we cry when we're happy.

Chapter Thirty-three

I've just told Dad my plan.

'The Stegnjaaics' old inflatable plastic swimming pool,' I said. 'If nobody's shifted it from where I left it, it's down there in the kiosk with all the empty plastic bottles. We could use it as a raft.'

Dad sighed and I felt his hot breath on my ear.

'It's got a huge rip in it,' he said. 'I checked it out the day the Stegnjaaics dumped it at the tip.'

We're floating in the blackness.

While Dad treads water I'm trying to think of another plan.

I can't.

My brain hasn't got another plan in it.

Not to save Dad.

Not to save anyone.

Not even to save me.

Suddenly drowning doesn't seem so bad after all.

Me and Dad, together.

Hang on.

Dad's body has just gone rigid.

'Empty plastic bottles?' he's saying. 'What empty plastic bottles?'

Chapter Thirty-four

Dad's a hero.

The Malleys and the Wilkinsons have been going round the campsite telling everyone how Dad saved us.

How he kept diving down into the pool kiosk and coming up with empty plastic bottles.

How he made us stuff the bottles inside our clothes until we could float.

How he tied us all together with strips of inflatable plastic swimming pool and towed us away from the diving board just before it collapsed.

OK, they reckon I'm a bit of a hero too.

I've tried to explain to everyone it was just luck that I'd stuffed the pistol from the boat down my shorts.

And luck that I had the idea of firing it while we were floating to attract attention.

And luck that it turned out to be a flare gun.

But people don't believe me.

Specially as Troy and Brent Malley are going round telling the other kids it wasn't luck, it was my guardian angel.

Mum's just tried to make me lie down in one of the army tents and get some sleep, but I don't feel like it cause I'm still too excited after being in the helicopter.

Plus it's too noisy to sleep with all those frogs making such a din.

Plus there's too much going on.

Mum understands cause she's pretty excited too.

She's got the plastic bags of bank money and she's giving a personal loan to whoever needs one, which is something she's always wanted to do.

I've been hugging Dad and Mum and Gran for about an hour.

Gran's spent a lot of that time gazing proudly at Dad, which I think is making him a bit nervous.

When Dad was voted chairman of the town clean-up committee, for a sec I thought Gran was going to call the newspapers.

Mr Bullock was behaving as though he wanted the job, until he saw Gran looking at him.

Then he backed away, though that could have been because Gran had just taken a drag on her cigarette and a mouthful of army biscuit.

Dad's just been explaining to everyone about government flood relief payments and how they're always more than drought relief.

While everyone was cheering, Dad put his arm round me.

He bent down and I thought it was for another hug.

It wasn't just for that.

'He's quite a bloke,' whispered Dad, 'your Doug.'

Why am I telling you all this, Doug?

Because in the helicopter I finally understood what you've been up to.

It started when I apologised to Carla.

'You were right,' I said. 'It was angel bull.'

She grinned, and her eyes were softer and happier than I'd ever seen.

'No, it wasn't,' she said.

And she opened the plastic bag from the boat and showed me the old notebook.

Her dad's notebook.

Carla wouldn't show me what was in it, but every time she peeked inside her eyes glowed softer so I reckon it must have been about her.

'If Doug hadn't made it rain so much,' she said quietly, 'I'd never have found this.'

I stared at her while everything sank in.

Carla hugged the notebook and smiled again.

'I've had a guardian angel all along,' she said.

So have I, Doug.
    He's over there with his arm round Mum.
    Thank you.

Water Wings

Chapter One

'What I need,' said Pearl, as she started to slide off the roof, 'is a grandmother.'

There weren't any around, so Pearl grabbed hold of the TV aerial instead.

Then a thought hit her.

She looked anxiously down at the driveway.

If she fell, she didn't want to fall on Winston.

He was the kindest bravest guinea pig in the whole world, but if he tried to catch her he'd also be the flattest.

Pearl could see him directly below, a fluffy black-and-white blob, peering up at her, nose twitching with concern.

'Winston,' she called, 'shift over there next to the herb tub.'

Winston didn't move.

He gave her a few encouraging squeaks.

Pearl braced her feet against the tin roof, gripped the aerial as hard as she could and leant out over the guttering so Winston could see her pointing at the clump of basil.

A gust of wind nearly blew her off.

'Winston,' she yelled, 'it's not safe. Move.'

Winston moved.

He hurled himself at the wall and tried to run up the drainpipe, feet scrabbling on the shiny paint.

Then he slowly slid back down.

Pearl couldn't help grinning, even though her heart was scrabbling inside her chest.

'Winston,' she croaked, 'forget what I said. Stay where you are, OK?'

Winston stayed.

Only his ears moved, trembling in the wind.

Pearl grinned even wider and felt her guts unclench.

What a dope.

He'd tried to rescue her.

Even though he didn't have ropes or pulleys or a fire truck with an extension ladder, he'd still tried to rescue her.

She wanted to climb down and hug him.

But first she had a job to do.

Mum's bra.

Pearl squinted across the roof.

There it was, flapping white against the chimney.

'Alright you dumb bra,' said Pearl, 'here I come.'

Legs trembling, she pushed herself up the sloping tin.

She could hear her shirt buttons scraping on the metal, and the rubber on her shoes squeaking like Winston when he got indignant.

'If you had a grandma,' Winston would be squeaking if he was up here now, 'you wouldn't have to risk your neck like this.'

Too right, thought Pearl, edging towards the dancing bra. If I had a grandma she'd teach me all sorts of stuff.

How to knit a jumper for a guinea pig.

How to write to Dad when I don't know where he lives.

How to peg Mum's bras on the line so they don't get blown onto the roof.

That's what Grandmas are for.

To teach you all the stuff busy Mums don't have time to.

Plus make you birthday cakes and help you get the guinea pig poo out of your hair and cuddle you once in a while and . . .

Pearl blinked hard.

This was no time to get distracted.

She wrapped an arm round the chimney and leant over as far as she could and grabbed the bra with her fingertips.

187

Just as well it's a 38D, thought Pearl.

She pitied kids with skinny mums. Grabbing small bras off windy roofs must be really hard.

She gripped the bra between her teeth and started to climb down.

A sports car that sounded like Mum's screeched round the corner at the end of the street.

Pearl squinted down.

Yes, it was Mum. There were only three red Capris in the whole town and Mum was the only one whose numberplate said CAR4ME.

Suddenly Pearl's heart started going scrabbly again.

There was a bloke sitting next to Mum.

It must be Howard.

'Winston,' Pearl called down excitedly. 'She's brought him home.'

Winston frowned at the approaching car.

'Don't be cross with her,' said Pearl. 'She had to wait a few weeks for the relationship to develop. New blokes can be put off if they find out there's a kid and a guinea pig.'

Winston's face softened.

As the car pulled up, Pearl peered at Howard.

He didn't look like he'd be put off too easily.

Pearl shivered with excitement and felt for the drainpipe with her feet.

'So, Pearl,' said Howard. 'This must be Winston.'

'That's right,' said Pearl.

Winston waddled across the carpet, sniffed Howard's squash shoe and gave it a friendly chew.

'Hello Winston,' said Howard, taking a step back. 'Haven't you got a cage then?'

Pearl left Winston to explain that he was a free-range guinea pig who liked to roam proud and unrestrained, plus when he did flake out it was in a hutch.

While Winston squeaked earnestly, Pearl checked Howard for grey hairs.

None on his head.

None on his legs either, what she could see of them between his squash socks and his shorts.

Excellent, thought Pearl. He can't be more than thirty-five.

Winston gave an impatient squeak.

OK Winston, calm down, she thought. I'm going to ask him the question now.

She took a deep breath.

Before she could speak, Mum came out of the bathroom in a towel.

'Pearl, don't pester Howard,' she said, rummaging in the washing basket. 'Let him have a shower. We're due at the restaurant in half an hour.'

Howard kissed Mum on the cheek and went into the bathroom.

Mum put her face close to Pearl's.

'He's the best thing that's happened to me since your Dad left,' she said. 'Don't blow it for me, OK?'

Pearl stared at her, puzzled.

Mum held a bra up in front of Pearl's face. It had sooty streaks on it, and a bit of dribble.

'Can't trust you with anything, can I?' said Mum.

Pearl sighed.

Nibble. Nibble. Nibble.

Pearl opened her eyes.

It was still dark.

Strange, she thought.

Winston hardly ever nibbled her ear in the dark. He usually waited till the sun was up and peeping through the dump trucks on her curtains.

Pearl sat up, straining to hear if the house was burning down.

It wasn't.

Then she heard Mum and Howard at the front door, giggling while Mum tried to get the key in the lock.

Pearl gave Winston a grateful kiss on the tummy.

'Thanks,' she whispered. 'I was out like a light. Dunno what I'd do without you Winston.'

Winston squeaked softly in her ear. Something about getting on with asking Howard the question and not wasting time being drippy.

'Good point,' Pearl whispered, and listened carefully as Mum and Howard banged the front door shut behind them.

After a bit she heard Mum go into her room and Howard clump into the bathroom.

Pearl slipped out of bed and crept along the hallway.

The bathroom door was open.

She peeped in.

Howard was at the sink, shirt unbuttoned, splashing Mum's eau de cologne under his arms.

'Howard,' said Pearl softly.

Howard jumped and dropped the bottle.

It smashed.

He spun round.

'Jeez!' he shouted. 'Don't creep up on a bloke like that.'

Pearl opened her mouth to apologise but it was too late. Mum was storming towards her, dress half undone.

'What are you doing out of bed?' she demanded.

Pearl started to tell her, then decided not to.

Mum wasn't even listening anyway, she was doing her speech about how parents who run busy offices for twelve hours a day deserve a couple of hours off at night without kids making them break the zips on their dresses.

Howard crouched down next to Pearl.

'Did you have a nightmare?' he asked.

'She doesn't have nightmares,' said Mum. 'I'm the one who has nightmares. That cologne cost sixty-eight dollars.'

Pearl sighed.

As soon as the toast popped up, Pearl put it on the plates and checked the rest of the tray.

Tomato juice, Coco Pops, scrambled eggs, strawberry milk and toast.

It was her first breakfast tray and she wanted it to be a good one.

'Shame there's no bacon,' she said. 'Still, this is almost as good, eh?'

Winston sniffed the fish fingers and looked doubtful.

'OK,' said Pearl, 'I know you think they'd prefer frozen peas and sweetcorn, but not everyone likes that as much as you.'

Pearl picked up the tray and carried it carefully to Mum's room.

She peered in.

Good.

Mum and Howard were still asleep.

'Remember,' she whispered to Winston, 'if

Mum wakes up we're just bringing her a breakfast tray, OK?'

Winston squeaked OK.

Good on you Winston, thought Pearl. Winston'd never dob on her, not even if he was being tortured with bulldog clips on his whiskers.

She pushed the door open with her bottom and carried the tray over to where Howard lay on his tummy, face half buried in the pillow.

She knelt down and put her face close to his ear.

'Howard,' she whispered, 'I need to ask you something.'

'Mmmmmpflbbb,' moaned Howard.

'Your mum . . . is she still alive?'

'Ggggnslfff,' groaned Howard.

'The reason I'm asking,' continued Pearl, 'is cause my mum and dad's parents died before I was born, so I haven't got an actual real grandma of my own but if your mum's still alive she'd technically be my grandma, as long as you and Mum are serious about each other.'

Pearl noticed the smudges of lipstick on Howard's face.

It looked like he and Mum were serious about each other all right.

'So,' whispered Pearl urgently, 'is she dead yet?'

'Zzzzgnkkk,' gurgled Howard, and his arm slipped off the edge of the bed and fell into the scrambled eggs.

His eyes snapped open.

'Ow!' he yelled.

He pulled his burnt hand off the plate, knocking a glass of tomato juice over Winston.

Pearl watched horrified as Winston gave a loud squeak, leaped off the tray and burrowed under the bedclothes.

'Arghhh!' screamed Mum, sitting up wildly. 'It's a snake!'

Winston peered out indignantly from the bottom of the sheet.

Pearl grabbed him and held him close to her.

There was a long silence while Mum and Howard stared bleary-eyed around the room.

Finally they focused on Pearl.

'Breakfast in bed,' Pearl said weakly, pointing to the tray. 'Hope you like fish fingers.'

There was another long silence while Mum and Howard stared at the tray.

'Jeez,' said Howard at last. 'Pretty noisy room service. I reckon most of Australia's awake now. Including my mother and she's sixty-eight and going deaf.'

Pearl and Winston looked at each other delightedly.

Pearl had a wonderful vision of the delicious

breakfast trays they'd soon be sharing in bed with their new grandma.

Homemade cakes, probably.

Maybe even homemade Coco Pops.

And cow weed scones for Winston.

A noise interrupted Pearl's thoughts.

It was Mum sighing crossly.

'Next time you get a bright idea like this,' said Mum, 'check with me first. And you know I don't allow that animal in here.'

Winston waddled out of the room.

Pearl followed, trying very hard not to do cartwheels.

Chapter Two

'Two thousand kilometres?'

Pearl stared at Mum in horror.

'She lives way out in Woop Woop,' said Mum absently, sipping her coffee and running her eyes over some business papers. 'Howard hasn't seen her for yonks. Eat your breakfast or you'll be late for thingy.'

'School,' said Pearl sadly.

She put another spoonful of Coco Pops into her mouth.

Disappointment made them taste like the dried sow-thistle she fed Winston for his bowels.

It wasn't fair.

All her life she'd waited for a grandma and now she'd finally got one, the dopey old chook lived too far away.

Pearl saw Winston frowning at her.

'I know, I know,' she sighed. 'It's not her fault

where she lives. Just makes it a bit hard to invite
her to school open days, that's all.'

Mum grunted to herself and scribbled something onto a page of figures.

Winston gave Pearl a sympathetic look.

Except, she noticed, it wasn't the same as his
usual sympathetic look.

His cheeks were more scrunched, almost as if
he was in pain.

And he'd done a pee in the butter dish, which
he'd never done before.

'You OK?' asked Pearl.

She saw he hadn't touched his breakfast, not
the rolled oats or the dried fruit or the lucerne
fibre or the strawberry milk.

Winston gave her an 'I'm fine' squeak, but
Pearl knew he was just being brave.

A person was bound to be feeling a bit under
the weather when they'd just been half-drowned
in tomato juice.

From the shower came the distant sound of
Howard singing.

Winston gave a little shudder.

And that's not helping, thought Pearl.

Winston had never liked opera.

Winston gave a grunt and waggled his bottom
in the direction of the bathroom.

For a sec Pearl thought he was just being a
critic, then she realised he was trying to tell her

an idea.

A really good idea.

'Good on you Winston,' said Pearl. 'Spot on.'

Mum looked up irritably from her sales sheets.

'Did you say something?' she asked.

'I'm going to see if Howard wants to go to my school open day,' said Pearl.

Mum sighed wearily.

'Howard hasn't got time for open days,' she said. 'He's got a business to run. He's a vet. The only one in town, so he's very busy.'

Pearl stared at her.

How could a bloke be a vet when he didn't even know the difference between a cage and a hutch?

Pearl listened to Howard trying to hit a high note in the shower and felt glad Winston had never needed a vet.

No way would she leave him at the mercy of a bloke who'd spent all his training years at the opera.

'Anyway,' said Mum, 'you don't need Howard to go to the school open day because I'm going. When is it?'

'This morning,' said Pearl quietly. 'Ten o'clock.'

Mum sighed again and typed something into her electronic personal organiser.

Pearl took a deep breath.

'Mum,' she said, 'I know you're really busy so if you're not going to be able to make it, that's OK, but I'd rather know now.'

Mum frowned at her crossly.

'Pearl,' she said, 'watch my lips. I'll be there.'

'And this,' said Pearl proudly, pointing up at the wall, 'is my project on guinea pigs.'

She looked anxiously at the pages to make sure Mr Gallico had stuck them up in the right order.

Then she held her breath, waiting for a response.

Winston stared at the project and didn't say anything.

Perhaps he can't see it properly, thought Pearl.

She lifted Winston up a bit so his whole head was sticking out of her school bag.

Winston flattened his ears, which Pearl knew meant he was concentrating, and blinked at the pages.

Then he gave several low whistles.

Pearl breathed a sigh of relief.

It was always nerve-racking, having your work assessed by an expert.

Particularly when other kids and parents and grandparents were pointing and giggling.

'Pearl,' said a loud voice, 'I don't think I've met your guest.'

Pearl tried to slide Winston back inside her bag.

Too late.

Mr Gallico had snuck up on her behind the egg-carton tribal masks.

'Thank you Pearl,' he said, gesturing for her to hand Winston over.

Pearl froze, heart going frantic.

Last week when Mr Gallico had confiscated Ewan Foley's dart gun, he'd chucked it in the bin.

'Thank you, Pearl,' said Mr Gallico more loudly.

He reached down for Winston.

Before she let go, Pearl gave Winston a reassuring squeeze just to let him know that he wouldn't be spending more than two seconds in the bin, even if it got her expelled.

Winston gave a loud whistle.

It was almost a scream.

Pearl had never heard him do that before.

'Be gentle with him,' she begged. 'He's scared.'

She hoped desperately that Mr Gallico had a secret soft spot for guinea pigs. He might. He looked a bit like one himself.

Mr Gallico held Winston in a pudgy hand and they studied each other.

Then Mr Gallico looked sternly at Pearl.

'Is your mother here?' he asked.

'No,' said Pearl quietly. 'She must have got busy. She's a general manager.'

A woman standing nearby shook her head.

'We're all busy,' she muttered to her friend, 'but some of us put our kids first.'

Pearl saw that many of the parents and grandparents were nodding and looking at her pityingly.

'This is the busiest time of year for a tobacco co-op,' Pearl explained to them. 'All the farmers are sending their tobacco in for Mum to sell. If she neglects her job, this town could go broke.'

The parents and grandparents thought about this.

'The fact remains,' said Mr Gallico, 'open day is for family members and relatives, not pets.'

'Winston is a family member,' said Pearl. 'He's been in my family for years.'

'He's still an animal,' said Mr Gallico.

Pearl wished she could cover Winston's ears.

'He's a mammal,' she said. 'He's the same as everyone else here.'

She looked around at the parents and grandparents, hoping they'd agree.

They didn't.

Nor did Mr Gallico.

'There are many differences between animals and humans,' he said, voice rising with anger, 'one of them being where they go to the toilet.'

A titter ran round the classroom.

Pearl stared in horror at the liquid trickling through Mr Gallico's fingers.

She couldn't believe it.

Winston had never done that before.

Mr Gallico picked Winston up with his dry hand and thrust him at Pearl.

Before she could take him, Mr Gallico spotted a large wet patch on his trousers and let go too early.

Winston dropped to the floor.

The classroom echoed with the loudest squeal Pearl had ever heard.

For a sec she thought it was Mum slamming on her brakes in the playground.

But it wasn't, it was Winston.

Pearl grabbed the key from the herb tub, barged the front door open and sprinted into her room.

'Nearly there,' she panted to the school bag cradled in her arms.

Winston looked up at her gratefully.

Pearl stuffed fresh hay into the sleeping compartment of his hutch and laid him gently onto it.

'You're home now,' she said.

She watched him burrow in.

Her hands shook with relief.

It had been the worst afternoon of her life, even though Mr Gallico had apologised and said not to worry about the dry cleaning and had let Winston spend the rest of the day in a book box full of egg carton offcuts where he'd gone to sleep.

Which was pretty unusual for Winston.

Pearl had felt sick.

She'd just wanted the bell to ring so she could get him home.

Now she put her face close to the hutch.

'If you end up with a limp from this,' she said softly, 'we'll sue him.'

Winston squeaked his agreement.

Pearl peered at him even more closely.

Had his squeak sounded strange or was she just overanxious?

The phone rang.

Pearl ignored it.

Mum's voice boomed out through the answering machine.

'Sorry Pearl,' she said. 'Absolute chaos this end. I tried to get away this morning but some ciggie bigwigs turned up unexpectedly and I had to take them to lunch. I'm glad I did because . . .'

Pearl stopped listening.

All she could do was stare in horror.

In the hutch Winston had fallen onto his side, his legs stiff, his whole body trembling.

'Do you have an appointment?' asked the nurse.

Pearl, gasping for breath, held the plastic bowl with Winston in it under the nurse's nose.

She knew the nurse would understand when she saw Winston peeping out of the straw, sad and quivering and in pain.

The nurse gently pushed the bowl away.

'The vet has several people waiting,' she said. 'He'll see you as soon as he can.'

Pearl put the bowl onto the counter so she wouldn't jolt Winston when she blew her top.

'Please tell the vet it's an emergency,' she said, 'and if he doesn't come now, Mum won't ever let him use her deodorant again.'

The waiting room fell silent.

Three people, two budgerigars and a German shepherd stared at Pearl.

The nurse obviously didn't know Mum.

Instead of saying 'she'd be too busy to notice', the nurse picked up the phone and spoke to Howard.

The next ten minutes felt like ten hours.

First Howard finished examining a ginger cat.

Then he told Pearl to stay in the waiting room while he took Winston into his surgery.

Pearl stood outside the surgery door, straining to hear what was going on inside.

She'd just started to apologise to the people and the budgies and the German shepherd when she heard Winston squeal.

She flung herself into the surgery.

Winston was lying on a table, trembling.

Howard was holding a glass tube against his white sleeve and studying the liquid in it.

He looked up, startled.

'Jeez,' he said crossly. 'Do you want me to drop this one as well?'

'Is Winston OK?' asked Pearl.

Her throat felt so desperate she could hardly force the words out.

Winston gave her a pleading look.

Pearl hoped it was just because Howard had been singing.

Howard put the glass tube down.

'How old is Winston?' he asked.

'Six,' said Pearl. 'Seven on August the nineteenth. Dad gave him to me for my birthday, just before he left.'

Howard sat down at his desk and started writing on a pad.

'As guinea pigs become temporally advanced,' he said, 'they can develop a bilateral renal nephrosis. There can be tubular atrophy, interstitial fibrosis and sometimes acute neoplasia.'

Pearl stared at him.

This was worse than Japanese at school.

Howard looked up at her and his face softened.

'I'll send Winston's wee off for tests to make sure,' he said, 'but I think you're going to have to be a very brave girl. It looks like his kidneys are pretty serious.'

Pearl's head was ringing with panic.

'You mean,' she heard herself croak, 'he's got to have a kidney transplant?'

Howard shook his head.

Pearl felt relief flood through her.

Winston looked pretty relieved too.

'Guinea pigs can't have kidney transplants,' said Howard. 'When renal disease is this advanced, it's time to say goodbye.'

Pearl gaped at him.

He was speaking Japanese again.

'Winston won't suffer,' said Howard softly. 'Two little needles and he won't feel any more pain.'

Pearl stood frozen for a long time.

Then she gently picked Winston up, kissed him, and ran out of the surgery with him as fast as she could.

Chapter Three

'Leeks?' said Craigette Benson, twisting her bedroom curtains in her hands. 'We haven't got any leeks.'

'OK, green capsicums,' said Pearl desperately, chopping broccoli as fast as she could. 'Green capsicums are good for the kidneys.'

Craigette didn't move.

'Come on,' pleaded Pearl. 'Your Dad's got a fruit shop. Look in the fridge.'

'You've had everything from the fridge,' said Craigette miserably. 'There's nothing green left in the fridge except lime cordial.'

Pearl took a deep breath.

Stay calm, she told herself, for Winston's sake.

She stroked Winston's cheek.

'Don't worry,' she whispered to him, carefully placing some crumbs of broccoli next to his mouth. 'If you can't eat this, we'll get you some leeks.'

Winston didn't say anything.

He just lay on Craigette's bed shivering under the duvet.

'Don't promise him leeks,' said Craigette, 'cause there aren't any.'

Pearl saw that the shivering was getting worse.

She turned away so Winston wouldn't see her face if she panicked.

'Craigette, please,' she said. 'Winston urgently needs vitamins for his kidneys. We've got to find something he can eat.'

Craigette wasn't even paying attention. She was peering anxiously out of the window.

'My parents'll kill us if they find you here,' she said. 'I'm not even allowed to eat lollies in my room, let alone prepare vegies.'

Pearl felt a strong urge to hit Craigette with the chopping board.

Then she saw that Winston was ignoring the broccoli, just like he had the lettuce, french beans, bok choy, beetroot tops, celery, sweet corn and frozen peas.

'Come on,' she begged Winston. 'Eat something.'

'There's beetroot on my wallpaper,' said Craigette miserably. 'My parents'll kill us.'

She dabbed at the wall with a tissue.

Pearl put a crumb of broccoli on her finger and held it to Winston's lips.

'Just try one bit,' she said. 'If you're too weak to chew, just suck it.'

She held her breath, praying he would.

'Oh no,' moaned Craigette, 'celery in my slippers.'

Winston looked up at Pearl with moist eyes.

'And lettuce under my pillow,' said Craigette. 'Yuk.'

Pearl took a desperate breath.

What if Howard was right?

What if Winston wasn't going to get better?

In the distance the doorbell rang.

Craigette hurried out of the room.

That's all we need, thought Pearl. Angry parents who don't understand how dangerous yelling can be for a sick guinea pig.

She put her mouth close to Winston's ear.

'We've got to shift,' she said urgently. 'I'm taking you to ...'

She thought frantically.

'... to a shack in the bush. With an old stove so I can make you grass and thistle soup.'

While she tried to remember if she'd ever come across any shacks with working stoves within walking distance of town, Pearl began to gently lift Winston out from under the duvet.

He squealed with pain.

Heart scrabbling, Pearl slid him back under the cover and stroked his quivering fur.

He looked up at her anxiously.

'It's OK,' she said, her own throat aching with worry. 'Don't worry about Craigette's parents. Fruit shop owners have to help people with vitamin deficiencies, it's the law.'

She heard footsteps behind her and turned.

But it wasn't Mr and Mrs Benson.

It was Mum and Howard.

'It's a tragedy,' said Mum, overtaking an ambulance, 'and we feel for you, love. But we do not have time for these hide-and-seek games.'

'And it's not fair on Winston,' said Howard. 'He was in a lot of pain. You should be grateful your friend rang us.'

In the back seat Pearl didn't say anything.

She imagined a giant slug crawling out of a lettuce in the fruit shop and eating Craigette.

It didn't make her feel any better, so she went back to concentrating on how Winston was feeling.

He lay on her lap, his head cradled in her hands.

Not moving.

'That injection,' said Pearl, 'was just to make him feel better, right?'

'Yes,' said Howard patiently, 'it was just to control the pain.'

Pearl didn't take her eyes off Winston.

You'd better be telling the truth, she thought.

She wondered how many horse tranquillisers it would take to kill a vet.

'Pearl,' said Mum, 'I've been thinking. How would you like a mobile phone?'

'If Howard wants to kill Winston,' said Pearl, 'he'll have to kill me first.'

'OK,' said Mum, 'it was just a suggestion.'

Pearl knew it was hopeless as soon as she saw the long words on the lab report.

Hands shaking, she went over to the surgery table and showed the print-out to Winston.

He looked at it and then looked up at her.

She could tell he understood.

Howard put his arm round Pearl's shoulder.

'Think of it this way,' he said softly. 'With a wonderful owner like you he's hardly suffered in his whole life. Shame to make him start now, just for the sake of a couple of weeks.'

Pearl tried to ask Howard if there was any way of transplanting something from her body to Winston's, but she couldn't speak.

'Because that's all it'd be,' he said. 'A couple of weeks of pointless pain and misery.'

The sadness in her throat was almost choking her.

'Or I can put him gently to sleep,' said Howard, 'and he won't feel a thing. Which do you think he'd prefer?'

Winston gave a tiny squeak.

Pearl looked into his pleading eyes and saw his answer.

But she had to be sure.

She pressed her lips against the fur on his cheek and strained to hear if he was squeaking anything about wanting heaps more vitamins or a shack in the bush.

He wasn't.

Pearl said goodbye quickly.

She was worried the first injection would wear off and she didn't want to risk Winston being in agony again.

Plus she didn't want to upset him with loads of crying.

It was bad enough for him knowing the second needle was waiting on the work surface.

So she just hugged him gently for a while and thanked him for being the best friend she'd ever had.

She could tell from his expression he felt the same about her.

Then Howard and the nurse came in.

'All ready?' said Howard.

Somehow Pearl made herself nod.

'Come on Pearl,' said the nurse, 'I'll make you a cup of tea.'

Pearl sat down and held Winston to her chest.

He blinked up at her gratefully.

She looked into his eyes.

'I'm sorry,' she whispered.

She saw that Winston understood.

'Do it now,' she said.

Afterwards, Mum arrived.

'You poor love,' she said, and put her arms round Pearl.

'She was very brave,' said the nurse.

'Not a tear,' said Howard.

'Takes after me,' said Mum.

Pearl didn't bother trying to tell Mum that she'd been crying for twenty minutes in the toilet.

She was too numb to speak.

'We'll have a funeral,' said Mum. 'Just as soon as I've dropped some clients off at the airport. Just you and me.'

'Where?' whispered Pearl, but Mum was already on her way to the carpark.

Pearl showed Winston the hole she'd dug.

'Sorry it's not much of a grave,' she said,

tilting him so his head pointed towards it.

She knew Winston couldn't actually see it, but showing him made her feel better.

Just a bit.

She was glad Winston couldn't see it because he'd probably feel offended at being buried in a herb tub.

'It was the only place I could dig,' she said. 'When Mum had the backyard brick paved to make it low maintenance, she didn't think to leave space for a grave.'

Pearl looked down the street for the hundredth time.

Still no Mum.

'Sorry it's not much of a funeral either,' she said. 'Mum must have been held up.'

She hugged Winston to her.

Even though he was going cold and stiff, his fur still smelt like Winston.

'At least I've got you for company,' she said.

But not for much longer.

Not once he was in the herb tub.

She stared at the dark damp hole for a long time.

Then she dried her tears.

'There's no way I'm putting you in there Winston,' she said.

She filled the hole in loosely so there was a mound and stuck in the cross she'd made from two of the roof supports from Winston's hutch.

Then she carried Winston into the kitchen, opened the freezer, and laid him carefully at the back under the peas and sweet corn he loved so much.

Chapter Four

'It's a crisis,' said Mum, plonking an armful of business papers and takeaway on the kitchen table. 'Barely two weeks till the Tobacco Carnival and the Carnival Queen writes her car off.'

Pearl tried to look sympathetic.

'Extensive whiplash,' said Mum. 'Doctor says she'll be in bed for a month. I asked him if there was any way we could prop her up on the float, but he said no chance.'

Mum sighed and stared at the paperwork, lost in thought.

Then she remembered something.

'Oh no,' she said, 'have I missed the funeral?'

Pearl nodded.

'Sorry,' said Mum.

She started unwrapping the takeaway.

'Let's eat,' she said, 'and then you can show

me where you've buried him. Do you want peas or corn with your burger?'

'I don't really feel like vegies,' said Pearl quietly, leaning against the freezer door.

'I was hoping you'd say that,' said Mum.

Mum stared at the herb tub, mouth open.

'There wasn't anywhere else to dig,' said Pearl.

'But . . . what about my herbs?' screeched Mum.

'I put them all back in,' said Pearl. 'They'll be fine. Things always grow extra well in grave-yards.'

Mum looked ill.

For a fleeting second Pearl was tempted to put Mum out of her misery and tell her to look in the freezer.

She didn't.

It'd be suicide.

Winston would probably end up in the garbage or somewhere.

'You could have buried him at school,' said Mum, exasperated. 'Or at Howard's place. He's got a big garden.'

Pearl blinked hard to keep the tears in.

Mum might have an important job, but she didn't know much about death.

Or daughters.

Pearl had just turned her light out and was about

to have a cry when Mum came in and sat on the bed.

She took Pearl's hand.

I don't believe it, thought Pearl. It's been years since she did anything like this.

Despite everything, Pearl felt a warm feeling creep into her chest.

It didn't stay long.

'What I've decided to do,' said Mum, 'is go to Sydney and sign up a Carnival Queen there. A soapie actor or something like that. I'm not risking another town girl.'

Pearl stared at Mum in the darkness.

'It'll only be for a few days,' said Mum. 'Howard's getting a locum in to mind the surgery and he's coming with me cause he's got a mate who works in telly. So we'll need to find someone for you to stay with. One of the girls at school.'

Pearl didn't say anything.

She bit her lip to stop herself.

It wouldn't be fair saying what she wanted to say to a mother with such a heavy workload.

But the words came out anyway.

'Mum,' said Pearl quietly. 'Don't go. I'm really sad and I need you.'

Mum gave an exasperated sigh.

'Love,' she said, 'I have to. You know how important the Tobacco Carnival is to this town. And to my job. Don't do this to me.'

'Sorry,' said Pearl.

Mum squeezed Pearl's hand so hard it hurt.

'You choose someone to stay with,' said Mum, 'OK?'

Pearl lay in the darkness for a long time and let thoughts run through her mind and tears run down her cheeks.

Then she switched on her light and looked for a pen and some paper.

Dear Grandma, she wrote.

Hope you don't mind me calling you that, but as your son and my mum are going out together, I think it's the legal word.

Can I come and live with you?

I know this is a bit sudden, but there's nothing left for me here.

My best friend in the whole world died today which just leaves Mum and she's very busy and doesn't really have time for me. It's not her fault, it happens sometimes when you're a chief executive and sole breadwinner.

I haven't got any other grandmas or grandpas and Dad lives overseas somewhere but he won't tell us where.

I'm very good at breakfast trays, and am willing to learn embroidery and walking frame maintenance and anything else you might need a hand with.

Please reply soon and I'll come straight away.

Your new grand daughter,

Pearl Woziak

PS I can only come if you've got a freezer.

Pearl crept out to the kitchen to show Winston. The ice on his fur made him look old and grey and wise, and even though she knew he couldn't actually read what she'd written, she was sure he would have approved.

'Howard,' said Pearl, 'do you have your mother's full name and address? I want to invite her to my school open day next year.'

Mum snorted into her Chinese takeaway.

Howard grinned through a mouthful of fried rice.

'I can probably remember it,' he said. 'Don't hold your breath for a reply, though. Sometimes she takes months.'

'Oh,' said Pearl. 'OK, have you got her number? I'll give her a ring.'

'You probably won't get through at the moment,' said Howard. 'They were flooded out up there last week and the phone lines are still affected. You could fax my brother-in-law. He's with the bank up there and they can use the army line.'

Pearl thought about soldiers and loans officers reading her letter to Grandma.

'Thanks,' she said, 'but I'll post it.'

Mum snapped her fingers.

'Here's an idea,' she said to Howard. 'Your

mother could come and babysit Pearl while we're away.'

Pearl thought about this.

It'd be a good way to get to know Grandma before actually moving in with her.

Then she realised Howard was choking on a prawn.

'No chance,' he spluttered. 'Wouldn't get her down here with a bulldozer. She hates this town. Reckons she won't ever set foot here again.'

Pity, thought Pearl. Still, probably for the best. I'm looking for a permanent relationship and a new life, not a babysitter.

'Pity,' said Mum. 'We're not exactly being flooded with offers of accommodation from Pearl's friends.'

'OK Winston,' whispered Pearl, 'this is it.'

She looked up to make sure nobody was coming out of the post office, then lifted Winston out of her schoolbag and touched his nose onto the letter for good luck.

'Thanks Winston,' she said.

Winston had always liked to touch things with his warm nose for luck, and Pearl didn't see why this should change just because his nose was minus four degrees centigrade.

She took a step towards the post box.

'G'day Pearl, whatcha got there?'

Pearl's guts dropped to minus four degrees centigrade.

It was Craigette and some of the girls from school.

Pearl tried to slip Winston back into her schoolbag.

Too late.

They'd seen him.

'Jeez,' said Craigette, coming over, 'look at the size of that ice lolly.'

The girls crowded round.

'That's not an ice lolly.'

'It's hairy.'

'Give us a look.'

Then Craigette recognised Winston and screamed.

The rest of the girls stopped dead, eyes wide with horror.

Pearl was glad Winston couldn't see them.

'It's a perfectly normal scientific process,' she said indignantly. 'Heaps of people are frozen until medical science works out how to cure them in the future. You can pat him if you like.'

The girls backed away.

'You're sick,' said Craigette.

'Yuk,' said one of the other girls to Craigette, 'and you let her into your house.'

'Never again,' said Craigette.

Pearl watched them hurry away down the street making loud retching noises and giving her disgusted looks.

Then she touched Winston's nose on the letter again for double luck.

'We're going to need it,' said Pearl. 'Grandma's our last hope.'

Chapter Five

'It's been a week and still no reply,' said Pearl miserably. 'I guess she doesn't want me.'

She stroked the frost off Winston's eyebrows.

She knew he'd give her a sympathetic look if he could.

And a cheery squeak.

Pearl tried to cheer herself up.

Perhaps Grandma never got the letter, she thought. Perhaps her postman was swept away by a mud slide.

It didn't work.

She still felt miserable.

'If she was going to answer she'd have done it by now,' Pearl said gloomily.

For a sec she thought she saw a glint in Winston's eye.

The old glint he used to give her when he

thought she was being a pain in the guts.

Then she realised it was just the reflection of the frozen peas and sweet corn.

'Sorry to go on like this, Winston,' she said, removing a small icicle from his ear, 'but you're the only one I can talk to. None of the kids at school are speaking to me. Not since Craigette spread the rumour I'm a vampire.'

Pearl heard the front door bang.

She froze.

Mum was home.

'Pearl,' called Mum, 'what are you doing with your head in the freezer?'

Pearl quickly kissed Winston goodbye and slipped him under the bags of frozen peas and sweet corn.

She closed the freezer door just as Mum came in.

Pearl started to explain that she'd just been trying to cheer herself up, hoping that Mum would think she'd been looking for icypoles.

Then she saw Mum wasn't listening.

'. . . Howard couldn't believe it,' Mum was saying.

Couldn't believe what, thought Pearl, that some cages are called hutches?

'His mother announcing that she's coming down, just like that,' said Mum. 'She hasn't been down here for years.'

Pearl stared at Mum, heart thumping.

'She must have liked your letter, or whatever you sent her,' said Mum. 'She arrives on Saturday.'

Pearl struggled to control herself.

'So,' said Mum, 'you've got a babysitter. Look happy, if it's not too much effort.'

Pearl looked happy.

It wasn't any effort at all.

The effort was in stopping herself from flinging the freezer open, grabbing Winston and dancing round the house with him.

'Pearl,' shouted Mum, 'where's my red bra?'

Pearl sighed.

She stuck her head out of her room and yelled 'In the dryer'.

Then she went back to her Grandma Check List.

Rocking chair with comfy embroidered cushion.

Check.

Crocheted blanket with roses on it.

Pearl looked at the roses more closely and decided they were brussel sprouts.

Never mind.

Check.

Fluffy slippers.

Check.

China tea pot with matching cups and almost-matching saucers.

Check.

Pearl sighed happily.

It was everything a grandma could want.

She felt like running back down to the Salvation Army depot and hugging everyone there for giving all this stuff to a poor frail old woman they hadn't even met.

She didn't, because she couldn't take her eyes off the rocking chair.

It was perfect, even though the varnish was a bit chipped.

She imagined Grandma in it, blanket over her knees, fluffy slippers snug on her feet, sipping tea, her kind old face beaming at Pearl.

Pearl would sit at Grandma's feet and put her head on Grandma's lap and Grandma would stroke her hair.

They'd be sitting by the window in a ray of warm sunlight.

Not too warm, in case Winston melted.

'Pearl,' yelled Mum, 'the red bra was in the drawer. I can't trust you with anything.'

Pearl hadn't been to the airport since arriving in town two years earlier.

She'd forgotten how noisy it could get when there was a plane on the tarmac revving its propellers.

'You watch out for Howard's mother while we check in,' shouted Mum, pushing Howard towards the counter. 'She's getting off the plane we're getting on.'

Pearl went and stood by the Arrivals/Departures door.

Her guts were scrabbling so fast and her heart was booming so loud she couldn't think straight.

This is ridiculous, she thought after a bit, I don't know what she looks like.

She decided to greet every kind-faced little old lady just in case.

Except none of the people coming through the door were kind-faced little old ladies.

Relax, Pearl said to herself. Frail old folk always wait till last to get off a plane so they can be helped down the steps.

She glanced over at the check-in counter to see if the airline had wheelchairs for really old and frail grandmas.

While Pearl's head was turned, a loud rasping noise echoed through the terminal. It sounded like one of the propellers had come off the plane and was skidding across the tarmac.

Towards her.

Pearl spun round.

The noise wasn't coming from skidding metal, it was coming from an elderly woman.

A broad-shouldered elderly woman with the sleeves of her dress rolled up and a large suitcase in each hand and a cigarette in her mouth which sprayed ash each time she coughed.

There was a skinny boy standing behind the woman, slapping her on the back. He was whacking her as hard as he could, but it didn't seem to be making much difference.

Poor bloke, thought Pearl, having a grandma like that. She wouldn't fit into fluffy slippers. She probably wouldn't even fit into a rocking chair. If she tried to stroke your hair she'd probably set it on fire.

The boy's grandma finally stopped coughing.

She put her suitcases down, adjusted her bosom and pushed the sleeves of her dress up over her biceps.

Then she grinned at Pearl.

'G'day,' she said, 'you must be Pearl. I'm Gran.'

They sat in the back of the taxi waiting for the driver to heave the bags into the boot.

Pearl tried not to look like she was sulking.

It wasn't easy.

Just my luck, she thought bitterly. Instead of a grandma I get a retired wrestler. Plus she brings her real grandkid with her so I won't even get a look in.

'Mitch was that excited on the plane,' said

Gran, 'I thought he was gunna poop himself.'

'Gran,' said Mitch, sounding embarrassed.

Pearl snuck a look at him round Gran's broad chest.

He was the thinnest kid she'd ever seen.

Pearl realised he was giving her a friendly grin.

At that moment Gran leant forward for a cough, so Pearl didn't have to grin back.

The driver got in and Pearl opened her mouth to tell him the address. Before she could, Gran slapped a big hand on the driver's shoulder.

'The lake,' she said.

She grinned at Pearl.

'Bit of sightseeing on the way.'

Pearl's guts tightened.

That's all I need, she thought. A grandma with no concept of how expensive taxis are.

'Mum only gave me five dollars,' she said.

Gran didn't hear.

She was squeezing one of Mitch's spindly knees.

'Only joshing,' she said to him. 'Sorry if I embarrassed you.'

Mitch grinned.

Gran grinned back and punched him in the shoulder.

Pearl sighed.

Chapter Six

Gran stood at the edge of the lake and stared out over the water.

'Hasn't changed a bit,' she said.

She stood lost in thought, puffing on a cigarette.

In the back of the taxi Pearl stared too.

At the meter.

Eleven dollars thirty.

She took a deep breath and wondered how she could get Gran and Mitch back in the cab.

Set fire to their suitcases?

From the look of Mitch he wouldn't care.

He was running excitedly through the lakeside mud and reeds towards a small beach.

When he reached it he pulled off most of his clothes and ran into the water.

'Hope he's got a towel,' said the driver, going back to his newspaper.

Pearl sighed and looked at the meter.

Eleven dollars fifty.

She wondered what the extra charge would be for dripping on a taxi seat.

Her calculation was interrupted by a loud rasping noise.

Gran was doubled over, coughing.

'Hope she's got a hanky,' said the driver, not looking up from his newspaper.

When Gran finally stopped coughing, the meter said twelve dollars twenty.

This is ridiculous, thought Pearl. At this rate we'll use up all the money Mum left for takeaway and we'll have to survive on guinea pig grain.

She peered across the lake.

Mitch wasn't to be seen.

Must be seeing how long he can hold his breath under water, thought Pearl wearily. Won't be long, with his skinny lungs.

She waited.

Any second now he'd be popping up, blue in the face and gasping.

She waited some more.

Then she got out of the taxi, starting to feel uneasy.

'Gran,' she said.

Gran was gazing out over the water again.

Must be remembering the floods, thought Pearl. Probably wishing she'd had lino instead of carpet.

'Gran,' shouted Pearl.

Gran looked round.

Pearl pointed to Mitch's clothes on the beach.

Gran squinted at them.

Then she dropped her cigarette and dashed through the reeds.

Pearl ran after her.

'Mitch,' Gran was shouting. 'You can't swim, you stupid idiot.'

She doubled up with another coughing fit.

Pearl sprinted past her and without stopping to take off any clothes, dived in.

She could tell the water was deep because it was freezing.

She opened her eyes and waited for them to get used to the murkiness.

Suddenly she saw movement.

She couldn't tell how far away it was, or even what it was.

Something thrashing around.

Please, she thought, let it be Mitch's arms and legs.

And if not, an old rotary clothes hoist in a swarm of mullet rather than a giant octopus.

Teeth chattering, Pearl tried to swim over for a closer look, but each time she kicked her legs they snapped straight, jarring her whole body.

Something was wrapped round her ankles.

She pushed herself deeper to shake it off.

Slimy tendrils brushed her face and cut into her armpit.

Then she remembered.

Chest weed.

She'd heard people talking about it.

Winston had heard them too.

If he wasn't in the freezer he'd have reminded her before she dived in.

They called it chest weed because it wrapped itself round the chests of swimmers, and the ones that drowned ended up with it growing inside their ribcages.

Pearl tore at it but her fingers slipped off.

It was like slimy birthday present ribbon but a million times stronger.

OK, she said silently to the weed. I'll do a deal. Let me go and I'll be grateful for Gran.

The weed didn't budge.

She kicked as hard as she could and felt it cutting into her waist.

Her heart was scrabbling.

She was running out of breath.

Then suddenly the water exploded and there were bubbles surging all around her.

Pearl saw a huge dark shape moving towards her through the water.

A whale?

A fridge full of energetic fish?

No, it was Gran.

Gran wasn't the only one coughing as she dragged them into the shallows.

Pearl knelt in the muddy water and coughed harder than she ever had in her life.

She coughed up water, bits of weed, half her guts it felt like.

When they'd all stopped, Gran grabbed Mitch by the neck.

'You dopey mongrel,' she roared, 'you know you can't swim.'

'I'm learning,' croaked Mitch. 'I can't learn on dry land, can I?'

Gran spat disgustedly into the water.

She reached into the sodden folds of her dress and pulled out an even more sodden packet of cigarettes.

'I'm beginning to reckon,' she rasped, squeezing the packet into pulp, 'that perhaps I shouldn't have brung you.'

Mitch looked so hurt that Pearl felt a bit sorry for him.

Even though he was an idiot.

Then Gran sighed and gave him a grin.

'Only joshing,' she said.

She turned to Pearl.

'And you,' she said. 'In your letter you sounded a right tragic case. Now I get here and find you're a hero.'

Before Pearl could answer, Gran clamped her in a painfully tight hug.

Pearl struggled to explain that she wasn't a tragic case, just a bit lonely, but Gran was squeezing her too hard.

From the shore came a quiet cough.

Pearl looked up.

It was the taxi driver.

'Hope you've got some dry money,' he said.

When Pearl came out of her room with dry clothes on, Mitch was in the rocking chair rubbing his hair with a towel.

He looked at her sheepishly.

'Thanks for trying to save me.'

'S'OK,' said Pearl. 'I'd have done it for anyone. Well, maybe not Craigette Benson.'

Mitch grinned.

Don't grin, thought Pearl, you don't even know who Craigette Benson is.

'Why did you go out so deep if you can't swim?' she asked.

'It's a long story,' said Mitch.

She saw he was watching her closely.

'For most of my life,' he said, 'I've had a guardian angel.'

Pearl stared at him.

Perhaps her ears were blocked with chest weed and she hadn't heard him properly.

'Doug's invisible,' continued Mitch, 'but he keeps an eye on me and stops me getting hurt.'

Pearl rolled her eyes.

That's all she needed.

A loony cousin.

She waited for him to go on, possibly about his visits to Mars, but he was staring at the towel, picking at a thread.

'Doesn't matter,' he said.

Pearl wondered if there was some medicine she should be giving him.

Gran came out of the bathroom with a towel round her and a cigarette in her mouth and her hair spiked up.

'Ripper shower,' she said. 'Water up our way's so full of mineral salts it's like washing in gravel.'

Her feet were making puddles on the carpet.

Pearl thought about offering her the fluffy slippers.

Not much point.

She'd only fit a couple of toes in.

Gran blew out smoke and had a cough.

Perhaps she's got a dry throat, thought Pearl.

'Would you like a cup of tea?' she asked, pointing to the almost-matching china tea set on the coffee table next to Mitch.

'I'd rather have a beer,' said Gran, rummaging in one of her suitcases.

Gran pulled out a plastic thermos and poured herself a beaker of what looked to Pearl like the brown stuff that had come out of Winston's bottom the time he'd eaten too much muesli.

'I have to guzzle this health sludge three times a day,' said Gran, taking a swig and grimacing. 'Yoghurt, bran, lecithin, kelp and some sort of pollen. Doc reckons it'll keep me healthy. It's pretty crook if I don't have something to wash it down.'

'Sorry,' said Pearl, feeling sick, 'Mum doesn't drink beer.'

'No worries,' said Gran, 'I'll pick up a slab later. Hey, top rocker.'

She went over to the rocking chair and stroked it admiringly.

Pearl took a deep breath.

'I got it for you,' she said quietly.

Gran beamed at her.

'That was very sweet Pearl, thank you.'

Mitch stood up.

'Be careful Gran,' he said. 'You don't want to hurt yourself like you did when you fell backwards off Geoff Nile's trail bike.'

Gran aimed a pretend swipe at him.

Then she licked her lips and rubbed her hands together.

'OK,' she said, 'let's give it a twirl.'

She squeezed herself into the chair and slowly

rocked back and forward, eyes closed, face glowing with pleasure.

'I could spend my last days in this little beauty,' she said, 'no risk.'

Pearl felt a grin creep across her own face.

She reached for the crocheted blanket.

Then, with a creak and a loud snap, the chair collapsed.

'Gran,' shouted Mitch.

Gran, speechless with astonishment, lay on her back among splintered wood and pieces of shattered tea set.

Then she roared with laughter.

Pearl stared, horrified.

Mitch started to laugh too.

Pearl ran into the kitchen.

She flung open the freezer door and stuck her head inside.

'It's a disaster, Winston,' she said. 'My only chance at a grandma and she's a monster.'

Pearl pressed Winston's frozen fur to her wet cheek.

'I don't know what we're going to do,' she whispered.

Winston's eye didn't glint.

He obviously didn't have any suggestions.

Chapter Seven

'Twenty-three minutes,' said Pearl indignantly.

She pressed her ear to the bedroom wall.

The shower was still running and Mitch was still singing the theme to 'Star Trek'.

'Twenty-three minutes he's been in there,' she said to Winston. 'Mum'll go spare when she gets back and sees the electricity bill.'

A tear rolled down Winston's cheek and plopped onto the bedspread.

Pearl picked him up anxiously.

'It's not that serious,' she said.

Then she realised it was just his ice melting.

'Come on,' she said sadly, 'better get you back to the freezer.'

She wrapped Winston in a clean T-shirt and hurried out into the hallway.

And stopped dead.

Gran was blocking the way.

Pearl could feel melting ice running down her arm.

She wished she'd wrapped Winston in something bigger.

A sheet or a raincoat.

Gran saw Pearl and smiled.

'Sorry his lordship's hogging the bathroom,' she said. 'We had a drought for eight years before the flood and he's never been in a shower that goes for longer than two minutes.'

Pearl clutched the T-shirt and desperately hoped she hadn't left any bits of Winston poking out.

Grans who broke rocking chairs and tea sets, even if they did pretend they were sorry later, weren't the sort of grans who'd understand about frozen guinea pigs.

Pearl had an awful vision of Winston in the garbage and Gran yelling about rodents.

Or even worse, in a casserole dish.

She'd heard about outback people. In droughts they ate anything that moved.

'Mitch,' yelled Gran. 'Out of that shower or I'll put a knot in the hot water pipe.'

Her eyesight must be going, thought Pearl gratefully. She hasn't even noticed I'm holding a soggy T-shirt.

Gran turned back to Pearl and pointed to the soggy T-shirt.

'When you've finished your washing,' she said, 'fancy giving me a hand? I've promised Mitch a swimming lesson this morning and I'm still feeling a bit tuckered out after our dip in the lake yesterday.'

Pearl desperately tried to think of an excuse.

She couldn't.

All she could think of was getting Winston to the kitchen before he completely defrosted.

'OK,' she said.

'Good-o,' said Gran, and wheezed into Mum's bedroom.

Pearl hurried down the hall.

'Relax,' she whispered to the T-shirt. 'She didn't see you.'

Pearl stood in the shallow end of the pool and wished she was somewhere else.

Bed.

The movies.

The dentist.

She glanced over at the wooden bench outside the changing rooms.

Gran waved encouragingly.

Oh well, thought Pearl, let's get it over with.

'Watch closely what I do with my arms and legs,' she said to Mitch, 'then you try it.'

She swam across the pool, weaving through the other swimmers.

Mitch watched closely.

Then he tried it.

After two strokes he sank.

'OK,' said Pearl, after he'd surfaced spluttering, 'watch carefully how I float.'

She floated on her back for thirty seconds.

Mitch watched closely.

Then he tried it.

After two seconds he sank.

While he surfaced spluttering, Pearl took a weary breath.

The pool didn't close for another six hours.

'OK,' she said, 'I'll hold you.'

Mitch lay back onto the water and Pearl held him under his shoulders.

'Yes!' he shouted. 'I'm floating. Gran, look.'

Gran waved encouragingly.

'Let go,' yelled Mitch.

Pearl sighed and let go.

Mitch sank.

'Mitch,' said Pearl, after he'd surfaced spluttering, 'I'm not a very good swimming teacher. Gran'd be much better.'

'It's not your fault,' said Mitch, digging water out of his ear. 'I've got heavy bones. Dad's the same. You're doing a really good job.'

'Thanks,' said Pearl.

She wondered what a bad job would be. Holding him under and drowning him?

'Anyway,' said Mitch, 'Gran shouldn't go into swimming pools. She's got a bad chest.'

'She managed OK in the lake,' said Pearl.

She turned towards the bench to plead with Gran to take over.

Gran was talking to one of the pool attendants.

At last, thought Pearl, she's bringing in a professional.

Gran came to the edge of the pool.

'I'm feeling a bit tuckered out,' she said, 'so I'm going home for a health sludge and a lie down. This nice bloke'll keep an eye on you both. Oo-roo.'

The pool attendant waved encouragingly.

Pearl sighed.

Gran gave them a thumbs up and walked off.

Pearl turned back to Mitch.

'Why do you want to learn to swim anyway?' she asked. 'Where you live there's a drought most of the time.'

'And floods the rest of the time,' said Mitch. 'That's why I've decided to devote my life to flood control. Floods wreak terrible havoc on sheep and soft furnishings and families. My family's been torn apart by one. Mum and Dad sent me down here with Gran cause there's poo floating in our main street and they're too busy coordinating the clean-up committee to keep an eye on me. I want to find a way of harnessing the power of floods and using it for the good of humanity and livestock and families.'

Pearl stared at him.

His eyes were shining with excitement and chlorine.

'If you're going to control floods,' she said, 'why do you need to be able to swim?'

Mitch grinned.

'For when I make mistakes.'

Pearl found herself grinning too.

It was exactly the sort of thing Winston would say.

'Let's try backstroke,' said Mitch.

Pearl did backstroke across the pool.

Mitch watched closely.

Then he tried it.

After two metres he sank.

Exasperated, Pearl waited for him to surface spluttering.

'Mitch,' she said. 'This guardian angel you reckon you've got. Why don't you ask him to keep you afloat?'

Mitch's face dropped.

'He's not around any more. Guardian angels are for little kids, see, and he was spending too much time looking after me and I was really worried there'd be little kids missing out, so I told him to nick off.'

He bit his lip and stared at a four year old doing backstroke.

'I really miss him, but.'

Pearl realised she was biting her lip too.

This is ridiculous, she thought.

He's a total loony.

Off with the fairies.

A sandbag short of a flood control barrier.

So how come I know how he feels?

Pearl dumped her swimming bag on her bedroom floor and dumped herself down next to it.

I'm going to stay here for the rest of my life, she thought, and be a shoe rack.

At least it won't be as exhausting as being a swimming teacher.

She heard Mitch in the kitchen telling Gran that the swimming lesson had lasted more than three hours.

'So can you swim?' she heard Gran ask.

Pearl shook her head.

'How about float?' she heard Gran ask.

Pearl shook her head.

'He can sink,' she muttered.

Then she smelt something.

She dragged herself to her feet, sniffing frantically, panic clawing inside her.

She could smell cooked peas and sweet corn.

And something else she didn't recognise.

She sprinted to the kitchen, heart scrabbling.

Gran was at the stove, shovelling food from the wok onto plates.

'G'day,' said Gran. 'I've done a bit of a stir-fry for tea. Found a few things in the freezer.'

Pearl stared at the peas and corn and nearly fainted.

Mixed in with them were small strips of pale meat.

Chapter Eight

Pearl felt her blood go cold. Even colder than Winston's had been until recently. Gran and Mitch were staring at her.

Then Gran started to laugh.

Even though the kitchen was spinning and Pearl felt like she was going to throw up, she still managed to calculate the number of years jail Gran would get for cooking a member of the family.

Twenty at least.

And an extra ten for laughing.

Then she realised Gran was shaking her and saying something.

'It's chicken,' Gran was shouting, eyes wet with mirth.

'Chicken?' Pearl heard herself say.

'Chicken,' said Gran.

Pearl flung open the freezer and rummaged

frantically through the apple pies and mini pizzas.

No Winston.

She turned back to Gran.

'If that's not Winston in the wok,' she demanded, 'where is he?'

Gran reached into the back of the freezer and opened a plastic salad crisper.

Inside lay Winston on a slice of bread.

Pearl felt relief flood through her.

'The ice was making his fur sodden,' said Gran, 'so I put him in there. The bread'll soak up the humidity and stop him going mouldy.'

She put a big sympathetic hand on Pearl's shoulder.

Shaking, Pearl picked up the crisper.

'We're feeling a bit tuckered out,' Pearl said with dignity, 'so we're going to our room for a lie down.'

Later, after Pearl's breathing was back to normal and she'd apologised to Winston for her relative's rudeness in making him move home without asking, there was a tap at her door.

Mitch poked his head in.

He was holding a plate of stir-fry.

'Do you want any?' he asked.

Pearl glared at him.

'Sorry,' he said, and went.

Pearl lay with Winston for a long time and

thought about a lot of things, including feral grans and mad cousins and becoming a vegetarian.

Later still, when Winston was starting to thaw, Pearl took him back to the freezer and tucked him in with a fresh slice of bread and said goodnight.

On her way back down the hall she heard a noise coming from Mum's room.

It sounded like more mirth.

Probably Gran still having a chuckle about my mistake, thought Pearl.

Then she realised it wasn't laughter.

It was sobbing.

The door was open a crack.

Pearl peered in.

Gran was sitting on the bed in a thick nightie, shoulders heaving, tears streaming.

Pearl stared, shocked.

Then she understood.

She tapped on the door, went in and put her hand on Gran's shoulder.

Gran looked up, startled.

'It's OK,' said Pearl. 'You don't have to be sad. Even though it was a tragedy Winston dying, he and I still have a pretty good relationship.'

She grabbed a handful of tissues from Mum's

bedside table and pushed them into Gran's hands.

Gran seemed confused.

Then she managed a small grin through her tears.

Phew, thought Pearl. Glad I spotted that. She might have been blubbing all night.

As Pearl watched Gran mop up with the tissues, she felt a small grin of her own bubble up inside her.

Who'd have guessed, she thought. A tough old chook like Gran getting upset over Winston.

For a fleeting second Pearl had a powerful urge.

She pushed it away.

Don't be a dope, she told herself.

Even when they are a bit soft-hearted and need cheering up, feral grans don't like kids trying to cuddle them.

Even later, just as Pearl was about to drop off, Gran came into her room.

'You asleep?' she whispered.

Fat chance of that, thought Pearl, with all the coughing you just did coming down the hall.

'Not quite,' she said.

'Want a chocolate crackle?' asked Gran.

Pearl sat up.

Gran, looming large in the light from the hallway, was holding a plate.

'I can't sleep sometimes,' said Gran, 'and a crackle or two seems to help.'

Trying not to smile, Pearl clicked on the bedside lamp and Gran sat on the bed.

'Dig in,' said Gran. 'Mind if I smoke?'

Pearl shook her head and took a bite of crackle.

It tasted a bit unusual.

'I put muesli in 'em,' said Gran through a mouthful, 'and a bit of kelp.'

Pearl decided she liked the taste.

'What's kelp?'

'Dried seaweed,' said Gran.

Pearl wished she hadn't asked.

But they still tasted OK.

'I like a bit of a midnight feast,' said Gran.

'Me too,' said Pearl.

She didn't mention it was the first time she'd ever had one with anybody over eleven.

'Should we invite Mitch?' she asked.

Please, she said silently, say no.

'No,' said Gran, 'I had one with him just before we left. More than one a week's not good for a kid.'

Pearl nodded happily to show she agreed and took another crackle.

'But,' said Gran, 'I hope you don't mind, I did bring fish.'

Pearl stared at her.

252

Fish?

With chocolate crackles?

'His actual name is Frank,' said Gran, 'but everyone calls him Fish cause he was a top swimmer.'

Pearl looked around the room.

'My husband,' said Gran. 'I couldn't bring him in person, of course, cause he died seven years ago.'

Pearl stared at Gran again.

She was starting to see where Mitch got being a loony from.

'How did you bring him then?' she asked cautiously.

Gran started laughing, and then choking on her crackle. Red in the face, she pointed over her shoulder.

For a scary sec Pearl thought she meant Fish was out in the hall.

Then she understood.

She whacked Gran on the back.

Gran had a coughing fit.

Bits of crackle pinged off Pearl's wardrobe.

'I saw what you were thinking,' wheezed Gran when she could finally speak. 'You were thinking I had a big freezer somewhere.'

Pearl nodded.

She hadn't been, but with this woman anything was possible.

Gran shook her head, then tapped it with her finger.

'He's in here,' she said. 'In my head. Not his actual body of course, cause then I'd have arms and legs sticking out my ears. But all the best bits of him. The bit of him, for example, that made him give up the chance to swim in the district championships cause I was having Howard's sister. The backflips he did down the main street when an Aussie swimmer won a gold medal at some Olympics. Millions of bits.'

Pearl smiled.

If I'd been Howard, she thought, with a dad like that, I wouldn't have wasted time at the boring old opera.

'I invite the old bloke to lots of things,' said Gran. 'Just like you probably invite Winston to lots of things.'

Pearl grinned and went to jump out of bed.

'Yeah,' she said, 'Good idea. I'll get him.'

Gran held Pearl's arm.

'I don't mean that poor frozen old carcass out there,' she said quietly. 'I mean the real Winston.'

Pearl was speechless.

Poor frozen old carcass?

'That is the real Winston,' she said indignantly. 'I should know, I . . .'

Gran was tapping her on the head.

'The best bits,' said Gran. 'What was the funniest thing he ever did?'

'Well ...' said Pearl doubtfully, 'one was when Mum had some clients to dinner and they were still here really late and making a lot of noise and Winston got over-tired and went into the bedroom where their coats were and tried to have sex with a fur jacket.'

Gran roared with laughter, then had a coughing fit.

Pearl whacked her on the back.

Bits of crackle pinged around the room.

'And what was the kindest thing?' spluttered Gran.

'The night Dad left,' said Pearl quietly. 'Winston came into bed without me asking him to and slept really close to my face and soaked up quite a lot of the tears.'

Gran nodded thoughtfully.

Then she told Pearl some more of Fish's best bits and Pearl told her lots more of Winston's and there was a fair amount of coughing and whacking.

'I'll never forget Fish's funeral,' said Gran, munching her half of the last crackle. 'He wanted his ashes scattered in his beloved municipal swimming pool, so we did. Trouble was, it was empty cause of the drought and the council cleaners swept it out the next day.'

Pearl stared, horrified.

Gran grinned.

'Don't reckon it mattered to him that much,' she said. 'He ended up on the tip and he always liked the view from there. Didn't matter to me cause I had all the bits of him I wanted up here.'

Gran tapped her head again.

'You planning to have a funeral for Winston?' she asked.

Pearl didn't answer.

'Let me know if you are,' said Gran. 'I'm pretty hot at organising funerals.'

Suddenly Pearl felt very tired.

She turned off the bedside lamp.

'I think we should stop now,' she said. 'Good night.'

Chapter Nine

P earl knew it was a dream, but it was still scary.

She and Winston were in the backyard watching Gran dig a hole with a big plastic spade.

At first Pearl thought it was going to be a swimming pool for Mitch.

Then the fruit shop van delivered a coffin.

Gran started complaining that the digging was making her fluffy slippers dirty and asked Pearl to take over.

'No!' screamed Pearl and woke up.

She could hear what sounded like a loud motor.

Oh no, she thought, Gran's got a mechanical digger.

Then she realised it was the blender.

Pearl staggered out to the kitchen.

Gran was standing at the sink pouring lumpy

brown goo from the blender into a glass.

'Want some health sludge?' she asked.

Pearl shuddered.

'No thanks,' she said, and hurried over to the freezer.

Winston was still lying on his slice of bread.

Pearl reached in and wiped some of the ice off his fur. She noticed that one of his ears was bent round at an angle. Carefully she straightened it.

It snapped off in her hand.

Pearl stared at it, horrified.

'Oh no,' she gasped. 'Winston, I'm sorry . . .'

'He didn't feel a thing,' said Gran softly, taking the ear from Pearl. 'Trust me.'

She dipped the edge of the ear into her glass of health sludge and stuck it back on Winston's head.

Then she closed the freezer door and leant against it.

Pearl wanted to push her out the way and run back to her room with Winston and hug him for hours.

Except she was terrified other bits might snap off.

'I've decided,' said Gran, 'that today's the day for getting rid of junk.'

Pearl got ready to wrestle Gran.

No way was she going to let Winston fall into

the clutches of a woman who reckoned he was junk.

'I've got some stuff stored over at Howard's place I haven't had a squiz at for a million years,' said Gran. 'Want to give me a hand?'

Pearl digested this.

Mitch wandered in, rubbing his hair with a towel.

'Today's a school day,' said Pearl. 'I've got to be there in twenty-five minutes.'

Gran swigged the health sludge.

'School'll be there tomorrow,' she said. 'How often does your Gran come to visit?'

'That's right,' grinned Mitch.

Pearl thought about Craigette Benson and the hilarious vampire graffiti she was probably scrawling in the girls' toilet at that moment.

I can't even take Winston to school to keep me company, thought Pearl. Not till his ear sets.

She looked at Gran.

'OK,' she said, 'but we're not going anywhere near the pet cemetery.'

It was a struggle, but finally they got the trapdoor open in the ceiling of Howard's spare bedroom and climbed into his roof cavity.

'Only tread on the beams,' wheezed Gran, 'or you'll fall through the ceiling and give Howard airconditioning he won't really want.'

Gran led the way along a beam through the dusty gloom.

Pearl felt cobwebs drag against her hair.

She sighed.

'Never a dull moment with Gran, eh?' whispered Mitch.

Don't know why he's so cheerful, thought Pearl gloomily. Doesn't he realise grans are meant to be dull? Dull and small and neat and cuddly with a strong preference for tea and scones and flower arranging rather than beer and chocolate crackles and funerals.

'Poop,' said Gran, and rubbed her head where she'd banged it on a roof support.

Pearl wondered if Gran banged her head much.

It would account for some of her behaviour.

'Hey-up,' said Gran. 'Here's the go.'

She was shining her torch at a pile of old wooden boxes.

Pearl did the same.

Spilling out of the boxes were dusty old toys, books, clothes, shoes and tyre inner tubes.

'Righto,' said Gran. 'Let's get all this shifted down and then we'll get a taxi to the tip.'

Pearl grabbed a box, then had a thought.

'Instead of dumping all this,' she said, 'why don't we give it to the Salvation Army. They fix this sort of stuff up and give it to kids.'

'OK,' said Gran. 'Good thought.'

They started dragging the boxes back along the beams.

Pearl had another thought.

'We should sort through it first,' she said. 'There might be some stuff you want to keep.'

'It's all going,' wheezed Gran.

Boy, thought Pearl, some people really don't want to remember their childhoods.

She wondered if she'd feel that way when she was ancient.

She had a sinking feeling she already did, so she made herself think about something else.

The tyre inner tubes were sticking out of her box. Now she was close to them, she wasn't sure if they were inner tubes. They were too small and fat and pink.

Pearl picked one up and realised what it was.

'Gran,' she said, 'are these floaties yours?'

Gran peered through the gloom.

'They're called water wings,' she said. 'Put them back.'

Pearl dragged the other one out.

'They're just what Mitch needs,' she said. 'Even he could float with these on.'

'Ripper,' said Mitch.

'No,' said Gran.

She snatched the water wings out of Pearl's hands.

At first Pearl assumed Gran was just being safety conscious. The rubber was cracking a bit in places.

Then she saw Gran's expression.

Pearl had never seen so much sadness on one face.

Not even on Winston's the night Dad left.

Gran's face was so creased Pearl was worried it would start cracking too.

Gran stared at the water wings for ages.

Then suddenly she bent forward into the torchlight and stuffed them angrily into her box of junk.

Her eyes, Pearl saw, were full of tears.

Pearl had never seen anyone drink beer so fast.

Three cans, gulp, gulp, gulp.

'It was the dust,' said Gran, wiping her mouth on the sleeve of her dress. 'That Salvo depot was almost as dusty as Howard's roof cavity.'

Then she went for a lie down.

Pearl went to see Mitch.

'Mitch,' she said, peering through the steam. 'can I have a word?'

'Do you mind,' squeaked Mitch. 'I'm in the shower!'

He tried to cover himself with the shampoo bottle.

'It's OK,' said Pearl, 'we're cousins.'

Mitch frantically tried to wrap himself in the shower curtain one-handed.

'Listen,' said Pearl. 'Why was Gran so upset about those water wings?'

'Dunno,' squeaked Mitch. 'Perhaps she was wishing she'd looked after them better. Now rack off.'

Pearl asked Winston what he thought.

Winston didn't seem that interested.

Not so much as a glint.

Then Pearl saw why.

His whiskers had fallen off.

'You poor thing,' she said. 'Here am I pestering you with other people's problems and you're suffering from terminal frostbite.'

She turned the temperature in the freezer down a bit and put another couple of slices of bread into his crisper.

But even while she was worrying about Winston, and wondering if he'd be better off in aluminium foil, she still couldn't forget about the water wings and that look on Gran's face.

Gran was lying on the bed in a cloud of smoke.

'Gran,' said Pearl, after she'd tapped on the door and crept in, 'can I tell you something?'

Gran stared at the ceiling and didn't answer.

I think that's probably a yes, thought Pearl.

'I just wanted to let you know that you don't

have to be too upset about your water wings being a bit perished cause the sports store in the main street sells them. I rang up and checked. They're plastic, not rubber and they're twenty-nine ninety-five.'

Gran didn't say anything for a while.

Then she blew smoke out so hard it almost reached the ceiling.

Oh dear, thought Pearl. They're too expensive.

Gran turned and looked at her with sad eyes.

It's a problem for old people, thought Pearl. They can't keep up with the cost of things.

'Is that why you were upset?' asked Pearl quietly.

Gran's big hand flew out and grabbed Pearl's arm.

Tight.

'I'm sixty-eight years old,' said Gran, 'and I've known you three days. Something you'll learn, young lady, is that people don't spill their guts about everything to people they've known three days.'

Pearl's heart was pounding and her arm was hurting.

She felt her eyes getting hot.

'Personal,' said Gran. 'Do you know what that means?'

Pearl nodded miserably.

'Good,' said Gran quietly, letting go of Pearl's arm. 'Now hop it.'

Pearl fled.

She threw herself down in her room.

OK Gran, she thought bitterly, have it your way. I won't ever care about you again.

Ever.

Then she realised something was digging into her face.

Something on the carpet.

She peered at it.

It was a piece of chocolate crackle.

Pearl sat up.

Oh no you don't Gran, she thought.

You're the only Gran I've got and you're not getting rid of me that easily.

I'm going to find out about those dumb water wings if it kills me.

Chapter Ten

Pearl's feet were killing her.

I bet I've never walked this far in my life, she thought wearily.

Nearly there.

She could see the old people's home at the top of the hill.

Keep going, she told herself. This is normal. You can't expect to solve a mystery without a bit of leg pain. If you stop for a rest now your legs'll go completely stiff and there probably isn't a vacant wheelchair for miles around.

She trudged on.

To take her mind off the stabbing pains, she added up the total distance she'd walked so far.

From the house to the Salvos depot must have been about one kilometre, though she'd used two kilometres of energy by running all the way in case someone else was in the middle of asking for the water wings.

Bursting into the shop and finding nobody was and getting them herself and flopping down on the kerb weak with relief had taken a bit of energy too.

But then spotting a name written on the water wings in faded ink and struggling to read the dodgy handwriting and finally working out it said Babs Cuncliffe had at least given her legs a rest.

From the Salvos to the post office must have been about half a kilometre.

Looking for a B Cuncliffe in the phone book and not finding one hadn't been a rest because she'd had to do it standing up.

From the post office to the cemetery had been another half a kilometre.

Walking around not finding a gravestone with Babs Cuncliffe on it had probably been two kilometres, not counting losing her temper and kicking a marble slab and hopping about for a bit.

From the cemetery to the Tobacco Co-op had been at least one-and-a-half kilometres.

Just as well she'd been able to have a long rest when she got there while Mum's secretary made a few enquiries in her capacity as vice-president of the Historical Society.

Because when Mum's secretary hung up the phone, she'd told Pearl that Miss Cuncliffe was living under her married name of Mrs Meadows in the Sunnyview Nursing Home near the airport.

Mum's office to the airport was four kilometres.

Which made the total for the day nine-and-a-half kilometres.

Pearl groaned again as she dragged herself up the nursing home driveway.

If Mrs Meadows can't solve the mystery of these dumb water wings, she thought, wincing with pain, I think I'll just check myself in and stay here till I'm old.

'Mrs Meadows?' said the woman in the office. 'She'll be delighted. She hasn't had a visitor all week. Come this way.'

Pearl followed the woman along a corridor that smelt almost as strong as the bathroom after Howard dropped Mum's cologne.

As they passed an open doorway, Pearl peeked in.

A very old man was lying on a bed surrounded by medical equipment with about six tubes connected to him.

Through a window he had a view of the airport.

Pearl shuddered.

Poor thing, she thought. He looks like he's being refuelled for take-off.

The office woman stopped outside a door, tapped on it, sang out 'Visitor, Mrs Meadows', pushed open the door, smiled at Pearl and hurried away.

Pearl held her breath and stepped into the room.

And stopped.

And stared.

Sitting up in bed smiling at her was the most perfect grandma she'd ever seen.

'Hello,' said Mrs Meadows, fluffing her curly grey hair and smoothing her lilac knitted bed-jacket and twinkling at Pearl with soft friendly eyes. 'What a lovely surprise.'

'Hello,' said Pearl, heart scrabbling.

They introduced themselves.

Mrs Meadows patted the bed.

'Come and sit down,' she smiled, 'and have some butter shortcake.'

Pearl did.

Boy, thought Pearl, they're lucky, whoever's got her for a grandma. Wonder if she's got any single sons about Mum's age?

Mrs Meadows patted Pearl's hand.

'You're a very kind girl,' said Mrs Meadows, 'to visit an old lady like me.'

Pearl glowed.

'I've brought something for you,' she said, digging into her jeans pockets.

Mrs Meadows twinkled with anticipation.

Pearl couldn't wait to see Mrs Meadows' face light up even more when she saw her pink rubber tubes from so long ago.

She handed Mrs Meadows the water wings.

Mrs Meadows looked at them for a long time.

Hope she doesn't get too emotional, thought Pearl. It's probably not good for a frail old soul like her.

Pearl watched anxiously.

Mrs Meadows didn't seem to be getting too emotional.

If anything, she was twinkling less.

She was even frowning a bit.

'Where did you get these?' she asked.

'I was helping my Gran clear some stuff out this morning,' said Pearl.

Mrs Meadows' face twisted into a snarl.

She threw the water wings at Pearl.

They bounced off Pearl's head and skidded across the floor.

'Flo Siberry?' spat Mrs Meadows. 'Flo Siberry's your Gran?'

Pearl sat stunned.

She forced her dazed brain into action.

Howard's name was Elyard, which must be

Gran's married name. Siberry must be her maiden name.

'Your Gran,' hissed Mrs Meadows, sticking her angry glaring face close to Pearl's, 'killed my brother.'

Pearl gaped.

She slid off the bed and backed away.

The room was starting to wobble.

It's not possible, she thought. Gran's been flat out ever since she got here. She hasn't had time to kill anyone.

'She was fifteen when she did it,' growled Mrs Meadows. 'My brother was seventeen. He'd fallen in love with her, God knows why. Went round telling everyone she was going to be the Tobacco Carnival Queen of 1947 or whenever it was. She didn't stand a chance. She was too tall and she had a face like a boot.'

Maybe he told Gran that, thought Pearl wildly, and that's why she killed him.

'In those days,' continued Mrs Meadows bitterly, 'carnival queens had to do more than just wobble their bits. They had to be citizens and sportswomen. Flo Siberry couldn't even swim, so she asked my brother to teach her.'

Mrs Meadows' chin was trembling.

She wiped her nose on the sleeve of her bedjacket.

'He took my water wings,' she said, 'without

asking, and he and your gran snuck off to the lake together and he drowned.'

Pearl felt weak with relief.

An accident.

Gran wasn't a murderer.

Then she thought about what it must have been like for Gran.

Seeing her boyfriend drown.

Poor thing.

Pearl realised Mrs Meadows' chin was trembling again.

'I'm really sorry,' Pearl said.

Mrs Meadows didn't answer.

Pearl swallowed.

What else could she say?

'What was your brother's name?' she asked quietly.

Mrs Meadows glowered at Pearl.

'I never say his name,' she said. 'I never even think it.'

She opened a bedside drawer and took out a book. Opening it, she held up the bookmark.

Pearl saw what it was.

A wisp of hair.

'That's all I've got left of my brother,' hissed Mrs Meadows. 'That's all your grandmother left me.'

Pearl watched as Mrs Meadows pressed the hair angrily to her lips.

You poor thing, she thought. You've hung onto the wrong bit.

By the time Pearl got home her head was aching almost as much as her feet.

First I'll have a lie down, she thought wearily on the doorstep, and then I'll have a quiet chat with Gran.

'It was a disaster,' said a loud voice inside, 'an absolute disaster.'

Mum's voice.

Pearl took a deep breath and went in.

Mum and Howard and Gran and Mitch were having dinner.

Pearl hadn't realised it was that late.

'Hello,' she said.

They all said hello. Gran gave her arm a gentle squeeze.

'You're late home from school,' said Mum. 'I was just telling Mrs Elyard, the trip was a disaster. We found a soapie actress but she pulled out at the last minute. So it's back to local talent if they can keep their cars away from power poles.'

Gran put a plate in front of Pearl.

'Mrs Elyard has cooked us a wonderful dinner,' said Mum. 'Stir-fried lamb with some wonderful herbs. What are they, Flo?'

'Just chilli,' said Gran, 'and some basil from the

herb tub outside.'

Mum stopped chewing and ran for the bathroom.

While Howard put Mum to bed and gave her some indigestion tablets, Pearl had a long talk with Winston in the freezer.

She explained to him how she didn't want to end up like Mrs Meadows.

She could see he understood.

Then she went out to the front yard.

Mitch was in the street with the hose, watering the nature strip.

Gran was sitting on her suitcases having a smoke and staring at the stars.

'I'm gunna be staying over at Howard's,' she said. 'Just for a bit.'

Pearl took a deep breath.

'I want to have a funeral for Winston,' she said quietly.

Gran stood up slowly and looked at Pearl.

'I was hoping you would,' she said. 'That's why I saved these.'

She opened her suitcase and showed Pearl the pieces of broken rocking chair wrapped in her nightie.

'I don't understand,' said Pearl.

'From what I hear,' said Gran, 'Winston was a pretty special individual. I reckon he deserves a pretty special funeral. The Vikings, those ancient warriors from up north, when they were giving their heroes a send-off, they used to put 'em in a boat and send 'em out across the water in glorious flames.'

Pearl grinned.

A Viking funeral.

That sounded like Winston.

Gran rubbed her chin and looked at the pieces of wood.

'Hope we can build a boat from these that'll float.'

'These might help,' said Pearl, digging into her pockets.

She handed Gran the water wings.

Gran looked at her for a bit, then grinned.

Pearl was tempted to say more, but she decided not to.

Gran had made it pretty clear that some things were personal.

When they got to the lake, dawn was just starting to break.

'Hope you've got a torch,' said the taxi driver, reaching for his paper.

They carried the Viking ship with Winston in it down to the water's edge.

This time Pearl didn't say goodbye too quickly.

She didn't say goodbye at all.

She stroked Winston's fur, so dry and soft after she and Gran had blow-dried it, and explained some stuff.

How he mustn't be alarmed when he found he didn't have a body anymore.

How he'd find being inside her head much nicer than being inside a freezer.

How she'd always love him.

When she'd finished holding him to her lips, she laid him on the nest of twigs and leaves inside the boat.

Together, Pearl and Gran pushed the boat out onto the silver water.

For a few minutes they watched it slowly drift away, silhouetted against the pink dawn.

Then Gran squirted lighter fluid onto a twig and ignited it and hurled the flaming stick in a high arc.

It landed in the boat.

'I used to be good at darts,' said Gran.

Soon the boat was ablaze, moving out towards the centre of the lake.

Gran and Pearl sat down to watch it.

When Pearl's tears came, she laid her head in Gran's lap.

After a while she realised she wasn't the only one crying.

She squeezed Gran's hand.

Much later, when the last burning piece of

wood had slipped beneath the surface of the lake, and Pearl had thought up the best idea she'd ever had in her whole life, Gran was still stroking her hair.

Chapter Eleven

Mum and the rest of the Carnival Queen Selection Committee were pretty surprised when they yelled 'next' and Pearl and Gran walked in.

Pearl could tell they were surprised because their mouths were hanging open.

She waited for them to recover.

Mum was first.

'Pearl,' she hissed angrily, leaping to her feet, 'what are you doing here?'

The rest of the people round the boardroom table started to chuckle.

'Sorry, lovey,' said Mr Tucker, the president of the Tobacco Growers Association, to Pearl. 'You've got to be over fifteen to be Carnival Queen.'

'Bring her back in a few years,' said Mr Longbeach, the chairman of the Co-op board, to

Gran. 'When she's got all her teeth.'

Pearl opened her mouth to explain.

'No argument please, young lady,' said Mum, steering them towards the door. 'We're very busy here and you're not over fifteen.'

Pearl pointed to Gran.

'She is.'

Gran nodded. 'And I've got all my teeth,' she said.

Mum hesitated, confused.

Pearl pulled herself free and faced the committee.

'Tobacco's been keeping this town going for seventy years,' she said. 'It's been keeping Gran going almost as long.'

Pearl watched the committee take this in.

She could hear Gran wheezing quietly behind her.

Don't cough, Pearl pleaded silently, please don't cough.

'Tobacco growing,' she continued to the committee, 'is a traditional part of this town. Well, so's Gran. She was born here sixty-eight years ago. I reckon we should have a Carnival Queen who represents our proud traditions and ancient heritage and all the stuff that's made this town great.'

Pearl stopped, out of breath.

Gran smiled winningly at the committee.

The committee smiled nervously back.

Pearl saw that Mum's secretary, representing the Historical Society, was applauding silently at the rear of the room.

'Pearl,' said Mum, voice low with angry exasperation, 'I thought I told you to check your hare-brained ideas with me first.'

Pearl looked pleadingly at the committee.

'You know,' said Mr Longbeach thoughtfully, 'the lassie does have a point.'

Pearl was surprised they said yes so quickly.

Forty-five minutes, she thought happily, including hugging and handshaking time.

Not bad for a committee.

Mum sometimes complained that committees took three hours just to decide what biscuits they wanted.

After tea and biscuits (chocolate fingers) with only a small amount of coughing from Gran and no crumbs pinging off the boardroom walls, Mum led everyone out the back to the storage area.

'This,' said Mr Tucker, 'is it.'

Gran squeezed Pearl's arm excitedly as they looked up at a huge throne covered in gold-sprayed tobacco leaves.

'There's a matching canopy,' said Mr Tucker,

'and a couple of Nubian slaves'll be fanning you with big matching fans. I say Nubian, it'll actually be Ron and Les Piggott with boot polish on.'

'Sounds tops,' said Gran happily.

'The whole thing goes on the back of a semi-trailer,' said Mum, 'and you'll be up there for a good couple of hours. Will you be able to cope with that?'

'I'm stronger than I look,' said Gran.

She put her arm round Mr Tucker's waist and lifted him off the ground.

Everyone laughed.

Except Pearl.

Don't overdo it Gran, begged Pearl silently. Tobacco Queens aren't meant to have coughing fits.

Gran put Mr Tucker down and had a coughing fit.

Everyone thought she was putting it on and laughed even louder.

'One last thing,' said Mr Longbeach to Gran. 'You are sympathetic, I assume, to the nature of our industry.'

'You mean do I think tobacco growing's a good idea?' said Gran. 'Anyone got a smoke?'

When they got back to Howard's place, Gran put her arms round Pearl.

'Thanks,' she said quietly. 'You don't know what a ripper this is for me.'

I think I do, thought Pearl happily.

They stood for a moment, Gran holding Pearl's head against her chest.

With her ear pressed to Gran's dress, Pearl could hear that each of Gran's breaths was a wheeze.

Oh no, she thought. I hope Gran didn't get pneumonia yesterday sitting by the lake all that time.

Then she remembered reading that people with pneumonia also have temperatures and clammy skin and splitting headaches.

Phew.

Gran went off to get dinner on and Mum came in from the car.

'Howard's off tranquillising a horse,' said Mum. 'When he gets back, he and I have got a business dinner.'

Pearl nodded.

She could see there was something else Mum wanted to say.

'Sorry I grouched at you back there,' said Mum. 'Your heritage idea was a pretty good one actually. Certainly saved me a few headaches.'

She rummaged in her bag.

'I was too busy to get you a prezzie in Sydney,' she said, 'so get yourself something, OK?'

Pearl stared at the fifty-dollar note Mum had stuffed into her hand.

Boy, she thought sadly, Mum must be feeling really guilty.

'Thanks,' she said.

Don't feel guilty Mum, she thought. There's no need. I've got a gran to look after me.

After Mum had gone to make a phone call, Pearl went to find Mitch to tell him the good news about Gran and the carnival.

He wasn't in his room.

Then Pearl noticed the trapdoor in the ceiling was open.

She climbed up into the roof cavity.

Mitch was sitting on a beam in the gloom.

'You OK?' asked Pearl.

'I can't stop thinking about that poor bloke you told me about,' said Mitch. 'Gran's boy-friend who drowned. If only he'd had a guardian angel, he'd have been right.'

'Perhaps he did,' said Pearl. 'Perhaps it all happened so quickly he didn't have a chance to call his guardian angel.'

'Or perhaps,' said Mitch gloomily, 'he'd sent his guardian angel away to look after little kids.'

Pearl looked at Mitch's sad freckled face and wished there was something she could do to help him feel better.

She realised there was.

Later, after she'd told her idea to Mitch and he'd got excited, she ran through it in her head with Winston.

He thought it was good idea, too.

'I can't take all the credit,' said Pearl modestly. 'I reckon having a Gran helps a person think better.'

The new water wings were bright yellow.

Pearl felt a bit embarrassed putting them on because it was after six and the swimming club people were training in the pool.

She put them on anyway.

No point buying them for Mitch and not showing him how to use them.

She showed him how they worked much better for breaststroke than crawl, and how for backstroke they were suicide.

'Let me try,' said Mitch excitedly.

He sat on the side and Pearl helped him put a pair on his arms and the other pair on his legs.

The man in the sports shop had told her she'd only need one pair, but she'd told the man in the sports shop he didn't know Mitch.

He must have understood because he'd let her have both pairs for fifty dollars.

'Today,' said Pearl, when Mitch was ready to go, 'just stretch out your arms and legs and float.'

Mitch slipped into the water.

He thrashed around for a while with only his arms and legs above the surface.

Pearl wondered if he was going to be the first person in the history of the world to drown with four water wings on.

Then, suddenly, Mitch was on his back with his arms and legs straight out and nearly half his body out of the water.

'I'm floating!' he yelled.

The swimming club people all looked over and joined Pearl in the applause.

Mitch didn't care.

He stayed floating for a long time, face dreamy.

Then he kicked himself to the side and took the water wings off.

'I can do it without the wings now,' he said, 'I know I can.'

'Are you sure?' said Pearl doubtfully.

'Yes,' said Mitch.

He lay slowly back in the water, and sank.

As she came into the house, Pearl sniffed expectantly for dinner.

Nothing.

Must be the chlorine up my nose, she thought. Gran's probably up to her elbows in stir-fry in the kitchen at this very moment.

Pearl went into Howard's big kitchen.

Gran wasn't at the stove, she was sitting at the table and she looked terrible.

Her face was grey and her shoulders were slumped.

Pearl stared at her in alarm.

Then Pearl saw that Mum and Howard were standing up the other end of the table.

Mum was staring at Gran too.

Not in alarm, in exasperation.

'Is this true?' said Mum to Gran.

Slowly, Gran nodded.

Howard put his head into his hands.

What's going on, thought Pearl. What's wrong?

None of them had seen her.

'If you knew this,' said Mum to Gran, her voice sounding strange, 'what on earth possessed you to think you could be Carnival Queen?'

Before Gran could answer, Mitch burst into the kitchen waving the water wings.

'I can float,' he yelled. 'Pearl got me these and I can float. Let's put a pool next to your throne, Gran, and I can float on the float.'

There was a long silence while everyone looked at everyone else.

'What is it?' said Pearl at last.

'Mrs Elyard isn't going to be Carnival Queen,' said Mum quietly.

'Why not?' said Pearl.

She wanted to shout it.

There was another silence.

Mum bit her lip.

'Tell them,' said Gran.

'Doctor Unwin was at our dinner,' said Mum, looking at the fridge, 'and he told Howard something he thought Howard should know about his mother. How she'd been to his surgery this afternoon.'

Pearl stared anxiously at Gran.

Gran stared miserably at the kitchen table.

Oh no, thought Pearl. You poor thing. You have got pneumonia. Or at least a bad chest cold.

'Mrs Elyard asked the doctor for pain-killing drugs,' continued Mum. 'Because ... because ...'

Pearl's heart started scrabbling.

Mum was never lost for words.

'Because,' said Gran quietly, 'I've got lung cancer.'

Chapter Twelve

Pearl lost track of time.

People were talking, but she wasn't sure if it was for minutes or hours.

Gran seemed to be doing quite a bit of it.

About the flood up her way.

About the trip she made to the city with some of the other flooded-out people in an army plane.

About the medical tests she had done on the quiet while she was there.

About the doctor who told her she had lung cancer.

About the specialist who told her it was too far gone to be cured.

Then Mitch started crying and Howard started shouting about why hadn't Gran told people.

Dimly, Pearl heard Gran say 'I didn't want to upset everyone.'

Howard and Mum got upset and told her that was ridiculous.

They started talking about hospitals in Sydney and second opinions, but Pearl didn't follow much of what they were saying.

Because suddenly her mind was racing.

Suddenly she knew what had to happen.

'Wait!' she shouted.

The others stopped talking and stared at her.

'Why can't Gran still be Carnival Queen?' she said.

Mum took a very big breath and snatched Gran's cigarettes off the table.

'Because,' she said, 'the Tobacco Carnival is to celebrate the growing of, surprise, surprise, tobacco.'

She thrust the packet of cigarettes in Pearl's face.

Pearl read the words printed on it.

SMOKING CAUSES LUNG CANCER

'Exactly,' Pearl shouted. 'Everyone knows that. So why can't Gran still be Carnival Queen?'

Pearl lay on the floor, furious.

Why is it, she thought bitterly, that whenever there's an argument between grown-ups and kids, the grown-ups always send the kids to their rooms?

And if their rooms aren't available, to other people's rooms?

Pearl looked around Mitch's bedroom.

There wasn't even a Winston-sized cushion, so she couldn't even have a decent cry.

She could hear Mum and Howard out in the living room, Howard on the phone and Mum on her mobile, yelling at doctors and specialists and hospitals in Sydney.

On the bed Mitch blew his nose on the sheet.

'It's more important she get cured,' he said, 'than be in some dopey carnival.'

Pearl sat up.

If Mitch hadn't been looking so sad and waterlogged, she'd have given him a shake.

'That's the whole point,' she said. 'Being Carnival Queen could cure her. It'll lift her spirits. Give her lungs the strength to fight back.'

Mitch stared at her.

'You're mental,' he said. 'If being a carnival queen cured lung cancer, there'd be thousands of carnivals every day with busloads of queens.'

Pearl sighed.

Cousins could be real dopes sometimes.

'It only works,' she said, 'for people who've been dreaming of being one for fifty-three years.'

There was a tap on the door.

Gran came in.

She gave each of them a long hug.

'I'm sorry,' she said, 'for not spilling the beans earlier.'

'Some things are personal,' said Pearl quietly.

'Mitch,' said Gran, 'thanks for coming all this way with me. It's a real tonic having you around. Took some sweat to persuade your mum and dad to let you come, but I'm glad they did.'

Pearl watched as Mitch digested this.

'And Pearl,' said Gran, 'thanks for writing that letter and reminding me I had a home town and some stuff to do here.'

Pearl realised with a stab of panic that Gran seemed to be making some sort of farewell speech.

Gran put her arms round them both.

'I'm sorry,' she said, 'that I can't be your Gran for a whole lot longer, but that's the way the crackle crumbles.'

'Gran,' said Pearl fiercely, 'don't give up.'

'I've sent a message to Doug,' said Mitch. 'It might take a while to get to him, but as soon as he picks it up he'll be here to help cure you, I know.'

Gran sighed.

It came out as a wheeze.

'You're both champs,' she said.

'Gran,' said Pearl, 'if you could still be Carnival Queen, would you?'

Gran gave a tired grin.

'Course I would,' she said. 'But I know that's off the bookie's sheet now, and that's OK, it was a lovely thought. So instead I'm going outside for a smoke.'

Pearl stared at Gran.

She felt like ringing up the cigarette companies and telling them to put another notice on their packets.

SMOKING MAKES LUNG CANCER WORSE

Gran must have read her mind.

She gave another weary grin.

'I'm gunna die anyway,' she said, 'eh?'

Not if I can help it, thought Pearl.

Mr Benson finished tying a cauliflower to his bullbar and shook his head.

'Sorry,' he said, 'but by the time I've got all the produce on the back of the truck, and Craigette in her spinach costume, there won't be room for another person.'

'See,' said Craigette. 'I told you.'

Pearl resisted the temptation to dress Craigette for the carnival a day early with rotten tomatoes.

'Please Mr Benson,' she said, 'you could be saving an old lady's life.'

Mr Benson sighed.

'She wouldn't feel comfortable,' he said, tying a bunch of carrots to his rear vision mirror. 'The theme of the truck this year is spring vegies, which is why I'm going to the expense of doing Craigette in baby spinach rather than silver beet.

Wouldn't really work with an elderly person on board, eh?'

'See?' said Craigette.

The manager of Foley's Trucking and Haulage (A'asia) Pty Ltd finished hanging plastic streamers from the barbed wire on the top of his depot fence and shook his head.

'Sorry,' he said, 'but all our vehicles that aren't interstate are already booked for the parade.'

'I'd wash your trucks every Saturday morning,' said Pearl.

'Sorry,' said the manager, grinning.

Pearl resisted the temptation to stop holding his stepladder steady.

'Please,' she said, 'can't you take my name in case there's a cancellation?'

'I could,' said the manager, 'if you've got a thousand dollars deposit and a class six licence.'

Pearl sighed.

The taxi driver tucked his newspaper behind his sun visor and scratched his head.

'Run that past me again,' he said. 'What is it you want moved? Perhaps I can fit it in the boot.'

Pearl stuck her head inside the taxi so he could hear her better.

'A throne,' said Pearl. 'It's a lounge chair

really, with a big heavy curtain on it. And a senior citizen.'

The taxi driver looked at Pearl.

'We'd strap her down,' said Pearl. 'And use towels so the roof doesn't get scratched.'

The taxi driver stared at Pearl, then shook his head.

'Can't put things on the roof,' he said. 'Against regulations.'

'OK,' said Pearl, 'are you allowed to tow things? For special customers.'

The taxi driver frowned.

'I can tow,' he said, 'but only in emergencies.'

Pearl took a deep breath, leaned further into the taxi, and told him about Gran.

Chapter Thirteen

'You look beautiful, Gran,' said Pearl.

'Yeah,' said Mitch. 'You're easily the best-looking Carnival Queen.'

Gran grinned.

'Best-looking one in the Co-op carpark, anyway,' she said.

She twirled around so that Mum's living room curtains billowed out around her shoulders.

'Gold and orange aren't colours I wear a lot,' she panted, 'but what the heck, it's a special occasion.'

Pearl checked her watch.

'The parade should be leaving the sports oval now,' she said. 'They'll be here in five minutes.'

She felt Mitch nudging her.

Oops, she thought, almost forgot.

She reached into her schoolbag and lifted out the Viking helmet.

She checked that the toilet-roll horns were still stuck to the brass plant pot.

They were.

'There you go, Gran,' she said.

Gran put it on, eyes shining.

It's working, thought Pearl happily. She's looking stronger and healthier already.

If only Mum could be here to see this.

Then perhaps she'd understand why we're having to borrow her car.

Gran gripped Mitch's shoulder, climbed up onto the driver's seat of the Capri, planted her bottom on the head rest and practised waving.

No time to worry about Mum now, thought Pearl. The parade'll be here in four minutes.

She went round to the front of the car to see how the taxi driver was going with the towrope.

It was in place.

'Will it be strong enough?' asked Pearl anxiously.

'I could tow a bus with this,' said the taxi driver. 'Little open sports car'll be a snack, even with a large grandmother in it.'

Gran glared at him.

The taxi driver grinned at her and gave her a thumbs up.

Gran took a deep wheezy breath.

Stay calm Gran, begged Pearl silently. Don't

put a strain on your respiratory system.

The taxi driver checked the towrope connections.

'She's a remarkable woman,' he whispered to Pearl. 'Wish I could have done this for my Gran. So, when's your mum getting here?'

Pearl took a deep breath.

This was the moment she'd been dreading.

The moment when the whole plan could end up in the ashtray.

'She won't be,' said Pearl. 'She's got VIP guests to look after. It'll just be us.'

The taxi driver looked doubtful.

'Who's going to steer the Capri?' he said. 'You kids can't.'

For a sec Pearl thought Gran was going to have a coughing fit, but she was just clearing her throat.

'I've had my driving licence for forty-nine years,' she said.

The taxi driver still looked doubtful.

'Can you steer from up there?' he said.

Gran reached out and gripped the wheel.

'One hand for steering,' she said, 'one for waving. Now, could you get in the cab and start the meter please?'

The taxi driver didn't move.

'I hope you've got an ignition key,' he said, 'for that steering lock.'

Mitch gave Pearl a panicked look.

Pearl pulled Mum's spare key from her jeans pocket and handed it to the taxi driver.

Mitch still looked panicked.

Pearl realised why.

In the distance she could hear the rumble of trucks.

The parade was coming.

Pearl didn't get panicked.

Just a bit worried.

'What I'm worried about,' she said in her head to Winston, 'is that when the parade trucks see a taxi pull out in front of them towing a red sports car with two kids and a Viking gran in it, they might slam on their brakes and crash into each other and cause the parade to be cancelled and me and Mitch and Gran and the taxi driver to be arrested for obstructing traffic.'

In her head Pearl was relieved to see that Winston wasn't scampering around looking for somewhere to hide.

He was giving her his calm 'everything's going to be OK' look.

And it was.

At first.

As the taxi and the Capri pulled out in front of the parade, Pearl looked anxiously at the front truck.

The Carnival Queen was staring and pointing at them with her tobacco wand.

Ron and Les Piggott were waving their arms and shouting.

In Australian, not Nubian.

But the truck, and the rest of the parade behind it, kept on coming.

Pearl grinned up at Gran.

'Comfy?' she yelled.

Gran gave her a thumbs up.

Pearl had the thought that perhaps they should have strapped her in somehow. She tried to remember if the Vikings had used seatbelts.

But it was too late, the taxi was towing them round the corner into the main street.

Pearl gasped.

The crowd was huge.

At least ten deep on both sides of the street.

This is incredible, thought Pearl. Everyone in town must be here.

The cheer that went up was the loudest Pearl had ever heard, but when Gran started waving it got even louder.

People were laughing and shouting and pointing and clapping, and nobody seemed to have noticed there were two carnival queens.

Or if they had, they didn't care.

Pearl hoped the organisers were feeling the same way.

She checked to see if Gran needed a chocolate crackle to keep her energy up, but Gran seemed fine.

With her weatherbeaten face glowing with pleasure and the sun gleaming off her helmet, she looked like the carved figurehead on a Viking warship.

Indestructible, except at funerals.

Pearl hoped Gran's lungs were feeling the same way.

Halfway down the main street, Mitch tapped Pearl on the shoulder and leant forward and put his lips to her ear.

'I was wrong,' he shouted. 'This is exactly what Gran needs to keep her going till Doug gets here.'

Pearl grinned and nodded, but she didn't reply, partly because of the noise and partly because of what she'd just seen on the VIP viewing platform outside the supermarket.

Mum, very agitated, pointing at the Capri and talking loudly to a policeman.

She seemed to be urging the policeman to do something.

The policeman seemed to be saying no.

Pearl thought of Winston's lucky nose and made a wish.

That the policeman had come to the parade straight from shooting practice so his ears were still ringing so he couldn't hear people telling him to arrest their daughters.

Then Mitch gripped Pearl's shoulder and pointed to a man in a safari suit and a woman in shorts standing near Mum.

The man's mouth was open and the woman was clutching her stomach and they were both staring at Gran in horror.

'My parents have arrived,' shouted Mitch unhappily.

Pearl looked up at Gran.

She must have seen what was happening on the VIP platform too because suddenly she wasn't looking so indestructible.

Her shoulders were drooping and she was wheezing a lot.

Pearl gave her a chocolate crackle.

During the coughing fit that followed, Pearl wondered if that had been such a good idea.

Several people in the crowd reeled back with bits of chocolate crackle on their clothes.

But then Gran stopped coughing, and for the rest of her triumphant journey down the main street she had the broad shoulders and even broader grin, Pearl was delighted to see, of a woman whose lungs were probably getting better by the minute.

As they turned out of the main street, the cheers fading behind them, Gran slipped down into the driver's seat and turned to Pearl and Mitch with shining eyes.

'Thank you,' she wheezed, and pressed her wet face to theirs.

Pearl glowed.

It's worked, she thought. Nobody could be this happy and terminally ill.

After a long time, Gran stopped hugging them.

Mitch blinked and looked around.

'Where are we going?' he asked.

'To the showground,' said Pearl. 'It's where the parade ends.'

Mitch peered nervously ahead.

'Wouldn't we be better off going somewhere else?' he said. 'Where we're not, you know, expected.'

Pearl shook her head.

'We've got to face them sooner or later,' she said.

Mum and Howard and Mitch's parents were waiting at the showground.

As the Capri rolled through the gates, Pearl saw Mum's face and Pearl's guts started to roll too.

She'd never seen Mum so angry.

Mum dragged her out of the car even before it had completely stopped.

'How dare you?' shouted Mum. 'How dare you ruin my parade?'

'Do you know the penalties for car theft?' shouted Howard.

'How dare you make me a laughing stock in front of my clients?' shouted Mum.

'Jail, that's the penalty,' shouted Howard.

'Not just local clients, overseas clients,' shouted Mum.

'How do you think your mother would feel with you in jail?' shouted Howard.

'You selfish, selfish, selfish girl,' shouted Mum.

Pearl was dimly aware that Mitch was copping it from his parents.

Even though she was being shaken and deafened and sprayed with saliva, Pearl managed to glance over to see how he was.

Which is how she came to see Gran slumped motionless in the car, arm hanging over the door, face on the steering wheel.

Nobody shouted in the hospital waiting room.

Mum and Howard and Mitch's parents stared at the carpet, white-faced and silent.

Pearl wouldn't have cared if they had yelled.

All she cared about was Gran.

If I've made her worse, she thought, I'll never forgive myself.

She wondered if jails accepted people who

303

asked to be locked up for long sentences.

If they don't, she thought miserably, I'll do solitary confinement in my room for twenty years.

She could see that Mitch, sitting hunched between his parents, was feeling the same way.

When the doctor came in, Pearl was first on her feet.

'You can see her now,' said the doctor, 'but I have to warn you, she's very, very ill.'

Everyone followed the doctor.

'You stay here,' Mum snapped at Pearl.

No way, said Pearl to herself.

She followed them down the corridor at a distance.

When she got to Gran's room and peeked in, they were all standing round the bed looking at Gran, who was lying ashen-faced on a pile of pillows with several tubes connected to her.

'How are you feeling, Mum?' said Howard.

'Tops,' wheezed Gran. 'All except my body. It's a bit crook. In fact I reckon it's a goner.'

Mitch's mum took Gran's hand.

'Don't say that, Mum,' she said. 'Tomorrow morning you'll be in the air ambulance and by lunchtime you'll be in the hands of the best specialists in Australia.'

Gran took several deep wheezy breaths.

'You've all been wonderful,' she said, 'but

there's something I want to say to you all, and that specially includes Mitch and Pearl.'

Pearl realised Gran was beckoning to her.

She took a deep breath and walked into the room, trying not to meet any of the adults' eyes.

Gran beckoned her closer and took her and Mitch's hands.

'Thanks to my two wonderful grandchildren,' said Gran, 'today has been one of the best days of my life.'

Gran gave them both a painful grin.

Pearl was aware that the adults behind her were shuffling and muttering.

'And I reckon,' wheezed Gran, 'that's the best way to call it quits.'

'Nonsense Mum,' said Howard. 'You're going to be fine.'

'No, I'm not,' said Gran. 'So here's what I'm gunna do. You people in this room are all the people I love in the world. After I've said goodbye, and told you what sort of funeral I want, I'm gunna speak to the very nice people at this hospital and ask them to give me an injection somewhere where it doesn't hurt.'

The room was silent.

Pearl saw the adults glancing at each other, puzzled.

Then she realised Gran was looking straight at her.

'And after it's put me out of my misery, young lady,' said Gran with a tiny painful smile, 'I do not want to be kept in a freezer.'

Chapter Fourteen

L ater, after everyone had calmed down a bit and Mum had gone to the hospital canteen with Howard to get him a cup of tea for his migraine and Mitch's dad had gone to the pharmacy with Mitch's mum to get her some antacid for her stomach, Pearl crept back into Gran's room.

Gran was asleep.

Pearl sat by the bed.

Poor thing, she thought.

No wonder you're exhausted after all that mayhem.

People weeping at you.

Pleading with you.

Waving private hospital brochures in your face.

Shouting at each other to talk sense to you.

Not listening to you.

Gran stirred and took a couple of sharp breaths and something rattled in her chest.

Pearl hoped it wasn't confetti from the parade lodged in her windpipe.

'Have a cough, Gran,' she whispered. 'Get it out.'

Gran slept on.

Pearl looked at the clear liquid in the plastic tube running into the back of Gran's hand.

She hoped it was the strongest pain killer in the whole world.

That's the least those doctors can do, thought Pearl, after treating you like that.

Lecturing you.

Quoting hospital rules at you.

Patting your hand and telling you to think of your loving family and not be a selfish girl.

And not answering, thought Pearl sadly, as she watched the tiny muscles under Gran's eyes twitch with pain, one simple question.

'Can she be cured?' asked Pearl.

The two doctors dozing in front of the TV jumped several centimetres in their vinyl arm-chairs and spilled coffee on their trousers.

They blinked and looked around and saw Pearl.

And frowned.

'This rest area is for medical staff only,' said

308

one. 'Visitors have to go to the canteen.'

'But they don't have to eat the food,' said the other. 'Fortunately.'

They both chuckled.

Great, thought Pearl. Gran's life is in the hands of Kermit and Fozzy.

'I just want to know if she can be cured,' said Pearl. 'Please.'

'Who are we talking about?' said the first doctor.

'My Gran,' said Pearl. 'In Room 14.'

The doctors exchanged a glance.

'She's comfortable and sleeping peacefully,' said the first doctor.

'Can she be cured?' asked Pearl.

'The hospital she's going to tomorrow,' said the first doctor, 'has the best facilities in the country.'

'Can she be cured?' asked Pearl.

The doctors looked at each other.

'It's OK,' said Pearl. 'I can take it. I've already had one close family member die recently.'

The second doctor looked at Pearl.

'No,' he said, 'she can't be cured.'

I can take it, Pearl told herself.

I can take it.

But her hands couldn't.

They started shaking.

Then the rest of her couldn't either.

After she'd stopped shaking and convinced the doctors she was OK, Pearl crept back into Gran's room.

Mitch was sitting on the bed talking to Gran.

'I'm sending him messages every five minutes,' Mitch was saying. 'Doug's a busy bloke, but he's got to check in with his secretary sooner or later. Angels have to, it's in their contract.'

Gran smiled wearily.

'Mitch,' she said, 'there's something I have to tell you about Doug.'

'No,' said Mitch, jumping off the bed. 'Don't try and tell me that bull about Doug not being real.'

He turned angrily and saw Pearl.

'She's her own worst enemy,' he said. 'How's Doug meant to save her when she won't even believe in him?'

Pearl didn't know what to say.

'I believe in him,' said Gran, 'cause I know he's real.'

Mitch stared at Gran.

Gran patted the bed.

'Both of you,' she said.

They went over to the bed and sat and waited for Gran to struggle with a rattly breath.

'When I was a kid,' said Gran, 'my parents didn't like me. Dunno why.'

She took another rusty exhaust-pipe breath.

'I turned into a bit of a ratbag. Cause of that other people didn't like me much either. Then, when I was fifteen, I met a young bloke who did. Other people reckoned he was an idiot for wasting his time with me, but he told them to boil their heads. He cared about me. Dunno why, but he did. I'll give you an example. He reckoned I could be Carnival Queen. I knew I couldn't cause I was too tall and I had a face like a boot, but he reckoned I could. Then he drowned.'

Gran struggled with another breath.

'His name,' she said to Mitch, 'was Doug.'

Pearl watched as Mitch struggled with a breath himself.

'Later on, when you were a scared little kid, Mitch,' continued Gran, 'and I wanted to tell you about someone extra special who'd be keeping an eye out for you ... well ... I probably shouldn't have done, but I picked Doug.'

Gran struggled to put her hand on Mitch's arm.

With Pearl's help she managed it.

'The truth is Mitch,' said Gran, 'I don't know if Doug's an angel or not.'

Pearl held her breath while Mitch and Gran looked at each other.

'I'm sorry,' said Gran.

Mitch stood up.

'You might think Doug's just some dead bloke,' he said, eyes blazing with anger and hurt, 'but he's gunna save your life, you wait and see.'

He ran out of the room.

Gran gave a long rattly sigh.

'Poor kid,' she said, wiping her eyes. 'I'm a prize dope. I should have told him ages ago, not leave it till the end. My trouble is I don't like painful stuff. I'm an old coward.'

Pearl picked up one of Gran's big wrinkled hands.

'No you're not,' she said softly.

She held Gran's hand while Gran's breathing became slower and quieter.

When Gran had drifted into sleep, Pearl let tears fill her eyes and run down her cheeks.

She sat in the dark room like that for a long time, stroking Gran's hair until the adults came back.

Chapter Fifteen

'Stop that talk right now,' said Mum, the carton of takeaway in her hand trembling with anger, 'or I'll wash your mouth out with detergent.'

Pearl couldn't stop.

Even though she could see it was upsetting Howard, she couldn't stop for Gran's sake.

'If she wants to die,' said Pearl, 'she should be allowed to.'

Mum thumped the takeaway carton down onto the table. Beef chow mein splashed onto the wall.

'In case you've forgotten,' said Mum, 'she's Howard's mother. And I care a lot about her too and so should you.'

'That's why we have to help her,' said Pearl.

Howard reached across the table and poured himself another whisky.

'Don't talk about things you don't understand,' he said.

'We helped Winston,' said Pearl.

Howard coughed whisky into his fried rice.

'I'm warning you Pearl,' said Mum.

'Winston,' said Howard, 'was a guinea pig.'

Pearl wiped a piece of fried pork off her eyelid.

'You said it was a shame,' she said, 'to make him suffer a couple of weeks of pointless pain and misery, remember?'

'Howard's mother,' said Mum, 'is a person.'

'I know,' said Pearl.

She felt her voice wobble.

Don't start crying, she said to herself.

Gran needs you too much.

'Why can guinea pigs be saved from pointless pain and misery,' said Pearl, 'and not people?'

Howard banged his glass down onto the table. Whisky and soda splashed over the lemon chicken.

'Because doctors don't do that sort of thing,' he said. 'They can't. They're not allowed to.'

Pearl took a deep breath and looked at Howard.

'Then why don't you help her?'

'Because,' said Howard, his face dark with anguish, 'I'm a vet.'

'Pearl,' said Mum, 'go to your room.'

Pearl went to her room.

She stayed there until she heard Howard leave and Mum go to bed.

After that she stayed there another three hours, just to be on the safe side.

Then she crept into the kitchen and opened the fridge.

Sorry about the lumps, Gran, she thought as she stirred yoghurt and bran together in a glass, but I daren't use the blender.

And sorry there's no kelp or pollen.

She had the fleeting thought of ducking out the back and seeing if any of the herbs in the tub were flowering, but she decided not to.

If she was going to help Gran, it wasn't pollen she needed.

Howard's back door was unlocked.

Pearl tried to keep her sigh of relief as quiet as possible as she slipped inside.

Carefully she put the glass of health sludge on the table and shone her torch around the dark kitchen.

Please, she said to herself, please let it be in here and not under Howard's bed.

As her beam moved slowly round the room, dark shapes and wobbly shadows appeared and disappeared.

Pearl recognised the toaster and the micro-wave and the milk bottle carrier, but nothing that looked even remotely like a vet's bag.

She shone the torch over the whole room again.

It wasn't there.

That meant she'd have to go through the house looking for it.

A dark house she hardly knew.

With three adults asleep in it.

Pearl felt panic start to scrabble deep inside her.

It wasn't in her chest yet, but it was on its way.

She took a deep breath.

Winston, she thought.

What would you have done, Winston?

In her head Winston was looking at her with a familiar expression.

The expression he used when he was encour-aging her not to be such a dope.

Then it hit her.

Of course.

The fridge.

Vets always keep some of their drugs in the fridge so they don't go off.

Pearl tore the fridge door open and there, tinkling in the butter cooler, were small glass bottles.

Holding the torch close, she studied the labels. She didn't know what half the words meant.

If only, she thought desperately, animal drug manufacturers had to put the same warning notices on their labels as cigarette manufacturers did.

THIS PRODUCT KILLS GRANDMOTHERS
Something like that.

Then Pearl saw what she was looking for.

A label that said Horse Tranquilliser.

That should do it, thought Pearl.

Gran's big, but she's nowhere near as big as a horse.

Pearl snapped the plastic top off the bottle and tipped the liquid into the glass of health sludge.

Then she went looking for a spoon to give it a stir.

She was surprised how quietly she managed to slide the cutlery drawer open.

It was so quiet she was able to hear quite clearly someone opening the kitchen door and coming in behind her.

Pearl froze.

Then she swung round with the torch.

Standing there, blinking in the circle of light, was Mitch.

They looked at each other.

Pearl felt the panic fill her chest and rush up her throat.

She waited for Mitch to yell out for someone.

His parents.

Howard.

Doug.

But he didn't.

'I've been thinking,' he said, straightening his pyjama top.

'Yes?' croaked Pearl.

'I reckon if Doug was gunna save Gran, he'd have done it by now.'

Mitch took a deep stuttering breath.

Pearl saw he'd been crying.

'I reckon,' he said, 'poor old Gran's on her own.'

'No she's not,' said Pearl. 'She's got us.'

Chapter Sixteen

The hospital was almost deserted, but Pearl didn't want to take any chances.

Not when it was a matter of life and death.

She and Mitch stood in the bushes, thinking.

'Gran's window,' whispered Mitch. 'She never sleeps with her window closed.'

'Good on you,' whispered Pearl.

She made a silent wish that whoever in the town council had decided to build a single-storey hospital should be rewarded in their life by getting heaps of love from a gran and a guinea pig.

They found Gran's room by counting the windows.

Gran's window creaked a bit when Pearl pulled it open wider.

Pearl put her hand on Mitch's arm to stop him

climbing in until she'd checked it was Gran in the bed.

It was.

Gran's eyes were closed and her mouth was open and in the pale glow of the nightlight her face looked smaller than Pearl remembered.

As Pearl swung her leg over the windowsill, a thought stabbed into her and she almost dropped the glass of health sludge.

Perhaps Gran had died already.

Pearl tried to hope she had, for Gran's sake, but she couldn't do it.

Mitch clambered in and knocked a vase over.

Gran opened her eyes.

She looked at them for a while, wheezing softly, before she spoke.

'G'day,' she said.

Then she grinned.

'I was hoping you'd come.'

Pearl held out the sludge.

'We've brought you something,' she said.

'Yeah,' said Mitch.

Gran tried to chuckle, but it turned into a cough.

Pearl saw Gran's face crease with pain.

'Thanks,' said Gran, 'you're both champs, but I'm a bit past that now.'

'It's instead of the injection,' said Pearl.

Gran looked at them for a long time.

'You're not just champs,' she said at last, 'you're angels. But I'm pretty much past that too. No point getting you into trouble when nature's doing the job for us.'

Gran coughed again and Pearl watched help-lessly as Gran's face twisted in agony.

She held the glass closer to Gran.

'Drink it, please,' she said.

'We want to help you,' said Mitch.

Gran looked at them, panting painfully.

'I don't need you to help me cark it,' she said, 'but I could use a hand with the travel arrangements.'

When they got to the lake, dawn was just starting to break.

'All the best,' said the taxi driver softly.

Pearl realised he was speaking to all of them.

He touched Gran on the arm for a moment, then reached for the note Gran had written.

'If anyone comes,' he said, 'I'll have this ready.'

Pearl and Mitch helped Gran down to the water's edge.

'On my back,' wheezed Gran.

They lowered her into the water.

As Gran started to float, the hospital nightie billowing out around her, Pearl saw Gran's whole body relax.

'If you can manage it,' said Gran, 'I'd like to go to the middle.'

'I can manage it,' said Pearl.

'What about you, Mitch?' said Gran.

'I'll try,' said Mitch.

Pearl launched herself into the water, kicking gently, steering Gran out towards the centre of the lake.

She saw that Mitch was hanging on to the other side of Gran, face tense with concentration, kicking furiously.

'Not too hard Mitch,' croaked Gran, 'or we'll go round in circles.'

'Sorry,' panted Mitch.

They moved slowly through the silver water.

Pearl realised Gran wasn't wheezing any more, and when she spoke her voice was clear and soft.

'I'm not gunna say goodbye,' said Gran, 'cause you know where I'll be.'

Pearl nodded.

She glanced across at Mitch.

He was nodding too.

Gran didn't speak again, and when they finally arrived at the centre of the lake, the water fiery with the first rays, Pearl saw that Gran had stopped breathing.

Her face was calm and expectant, as if she was about to see someone she loved very much.

'Mitch,' said Pearl softly, 'it's time to let go.'

They let go.

Slowly, arms spreading in welcome, Gran slipped from sight.

Then Pearl remembered Mitch couldn't swim.

She looked anxiously over at him.

He wasn't thrashing around in distress.

He was on his back, gazing at the sky with an amazed, tear-streaked face.

Floating.

Pearl rolled over and floated next to him.

She closed her eyes and out of the warm darkness of her tears, two familiar faces appeared, smiling at her.

'Winston,' she said, 'I'd like you to meet Gran.'

In the distance Pearl could hear the sound of vehicles, and people shouting.

She took Mitch's hand and they headed for the shore.

Look out for more wacky adventures by

 ...

Misery Guts

Keith's heart was pounding. Calm down, he thought. You're not robbing a bank. You're just painting a fish and chip shop orange.

Keith is trying to cheer up his parents. But a pair of misery guts needs more than a pot of Tropical Mango Hi-Gloss to make them happy. What they really need, Keith decides, is to live in Paradise – trouble is, Paradise is halfway round the world. Even Keith Shipley is stumped by that one. Almost.

'Totally compelling' Children's Books of the Year

Worry Warts

Dear Mum and Dad,
This is just to let you know that I took the torch, the hammer,
the chocolate biscuits and the stuff that's missing from the
bathroom. So it's OK, you haven't been burgled. Please
don't worry, things are looking even better than I thought,
opal-wise.
Love, Keith

Going down a mine and digging up a fortune in precious
opals is Keith's solution to his parents' problems. Stacks of
money will save them from being permanent worry warts.
Won't it?

The hilarious, heartwarming sequel to *Misery Guts*.

'Readers can't get enough of him' *Independent*

Puppy Fat

'What section do you want to advertise in? Toys? Sporting equipment? Computer games?' The woman in the newspaper office took off her glasses and polished them on her cardigan. 'What are you advertising?'

'My parents,' said Keith.

Keith's worried. Can two single parents with saggy tummies and wobbly bottoms ever find happiness? Not a chance – unless he gets them into shape. Just as well Tracy the mountaineer and Aunty Bev the beautician are arriving from Australia . . .

The brilliantly bittersweet sequel to *Misery Guts* and *Worry Warts*.

A selected list of titles available from Macmillan Children's Books

The prices shown below are correct at the time of going to press.
However, Macmillan Publishers reserves the right to show new retail prices
on covers, which may differ from those previously advertised.

Morris Gleitzman

Blabber Mouth	ISBN-13: 978-0-330-39777-3	£4.99
	ISBN-10: 0-330-39777-X	
Misery Guts	ISBN-13:-978-0-330-39995-1	£4.99
	ISBN-10: 0-330-39995-0	
Puppy Fat	ISBN-13:-978-0-330-39997-5	£4.99
	ISBN-10: 0-330-39997-7	
Sticky Beak	ISBN-13:-978-0-330-39778-0	£4.99
	ISBN-10: 0-330-39778-8	
Worry Warts	ISBN-13:-978-0-330-39996-8	£4.99
	ISBN-10: 0-330-39996-99	

All Pan Macmillan titles can be ordered from our website,
www.panmacmillan.com, or from your local bookshop
and are also available by post from:

Bookpost, PO Box 29, Douglas, Isle of Man IM99 1BQ
Credit cards accepted. For details:
Telephone: 01624 677237
Fax: 01624 670923
Email: bookshop@enterprise.net
www.bookpost.co.uk

Free postage and packing in the United Kingdom